No kissing ALLOWED

MELISSA WEST

Entangled Publishing, LLC
2614 South Timberline Road
Suite 109
Fort Collins, CO 80525
Visit our website at www.entangledpublishing.com.

Embrace is an imprint of Entangled Publishing, LLC.

Edited by Kate Brauning
Cover design by Louisa Maggio
Cover art from iStock

Manufactured in the United States of America

First Edition July 2015

embrace

For my mom, who taught me the importance of family and remembering my roots.

Chapter One

So far tonight, I'd bought a random guy a drink, danced on a bar, and serenaded a girl during a karaoke song. And the night was still young.

"You're up again, Cammie," Lauren said, sliding a shot glass my way.

I tipped the shot back and then glanced down at the list, ignoring Grace's tapping on the bar. It was a scare tactic to make me question whether I wanted to take on the last task in our 10 Wild Acts Before Adulthood. But if anyone was going to win this game, it was me. I was fiercely competitive in everything I did. From sports to running times, to bets on who would graduate first, I was always in first place. Well, okay, maybe the graduating thing was because my last name came before theirs, and so technically, I had to walk first, but still, I was first. It counted.

And this was no different. I might not be the prettiest (Grace) or the funniest (Lauren), but I knew how to win, and I planned to win tonight.

It was the Saturday before our first real jobs—Grace as an assistant curator at the Met, Lauren a junior buyer for Bergdorf's, and me an account manager with Sanderson-Lowe, the top advertising agency in the world. And though I had always walked a straight line, never veering left for fear of failing, tonight I wanted to push myself. Have one crazy night before I threw myself headfirst into my career.

The only part of the night that gave me pause was when the girl took the lyrics of "I Kissed a Girl" too seriously and decided to throw herself at me as I came off the stage. After a moment of her kissing me with my eyes wide open, Lauren and Grace laughing hysterically beside me, I had to explain that while I thought lesbianism rocked, I didn't bat for the girls' team.

But now, I was staring at the final task on the list, my mind—and clearly my vision—blurry from one too many shots. "What does that say?"

Grace laughed as she swept her long black hair into a high ponytail, causing several of the guys around the bar to peer over. She was the sort of pretty that caused people to walk into things, which she used to her advantage as often as possible. I glanced up at her, waiting for her smirk to turn into actual words.

"Um…I'm waiting here."

Lauren grinned from beside me. "We made a last-minute addition to the list."

"Yeah," I said. "I figured that out when the *10 Wild Acts* suddenly had an *11*."

Lauren's grin widened, her bright red lips now stretching across her face. She refused to wear any other color of lipstick or gloss. Always red. And with her bleached blond hair and double-mascaraed lashes, she had a very Marilyn Monroe/Gwen Stefani thing going on.

I blinked hard, fighting to clear my foggy head. Obviously, they were going to make this as hard on me as possible. I eyed the list again, taking my time to read each excruciating word.

Hook up with a random guy.

A shiver crept down my back. I was twenty-three and I had never had a one-night stand—even a minor one. No awkward make-out sessions, no getting too drunk and losing control. My responsible side wouldn't allow me to take such a risk. And now…

Lauren bounced on her heels, and Grace had begun to do a little dance on her stool, causing more looks from the guys around us. I shook my shoulders out, trying to make it no big deal, when something occurred to me.

"You can't make additions to the list." We agreed on our ten things the weekend before, handshakes and all. They couldn't change it now.

"Of course we can," Grace said in a singsong voice, Lauren nodding along in agreement, and I knew I was outnumbered here. The real point to this whole thing became increasingly clear—they wanted me to step outside my shell. Take chances. Live. All words and phrases that would never describe me.

"Now, go find your guy. We'll even go easy on you and count kissing as hooking up."

"What? No. This is stupid, this—"

"All right then, she forfeits," Lauren said, winking at Grace. "It's just you and me now. Or you could just give me the hundred dollars, Grace. You don't need the money, anyway."

"No!" I said a little too loudly. Yeah, the shots were definitely taking effect. Dammit all to hell! Why couldn't I have shy friends, who thought dyeing my hair a different color was living? Oh, no. Instead, my best friends were both hard-wired to never get embarrassed, to never worry about the consequences of their actions.

Clearly, I needed new friends.

Closing my eyes, I told myself to stop being so ridiculous. If it was just a kiss, then I could do this. No big deal. I'd kissed plenty of guys. All right, *plenty* might be a stretch. Maybe five? But five counted as something. I wasn't a virgin, kissing or otherwise. Yet somehow, I'd never kissed a random guy. Never even had the urge.

I drew a breath. All I had to do was go up to a guy, start talking, and ask him to kiss me. Girls did that crap all the time, right? I could do this. Or I could just say no and lose. I mean, what was so wrong with losing? Nothing. I could lose. Cameron, the loser.

A sick feeling moved over me at the thought, followed immediately by sharp anger. Who was I kidding? I had never willingly lost at anything in my life. I wasn't a loser, which meant I had only one choice here.

Squeezing my eyes shut, I tapped my shot glass. "I need another. Scratch that. I need five more. Make them all doubles or triples or whatever. Just strong." I peeked back up at Lauren and Grace. "What sort of kiss are we talking about here? Because I've already been kissed tonight, so technically I—"

Lauren shook her head and pointed at the list. "Nice try,

but yeah, no. That chick kissing you doesn't count."

I started to argue just as a soft chuckle hit my ears, and instead of pleading my case, I whipped my head to the left to find a guy seated on the stool beside me, a white baseball cap with a giant, orange *T* pulled low over his eyes. University of Tennessee, hmm. I rarely saw guys in the city supporting teams from the south. It was usually the Yankees or Mets or Giants or whatever. He wore a button-down shirt rolled to his elbows, giving off a definite frat-boy vibe that me and my buzz had no patience for.

"This is a private conversation."

The guy grinned. "Well, then you might want to tell your voice that. Pretty sure the whole bar heard you."

My eyes widened before narrowing in on him. "Let me guess—fall retreat in New York City? Oh, how big and bad you all must feel."

This time he spun around to face me, leaning in so his scent hit me full force. And dear. Heaven. Above. I drew a breath, fighting the urge to sigh. Mild cologne, with a hint of soap. Entirely man. Entirely sexy.

Chocolate-brown eyes, framed in full, dark lashes, stared at me from below the bill of his hat, hints of dirty-blond hair peeking out at random—at his temples, tickling his neck. Suddenly, I wanted to take back all my words and begin again with, "Hi, I'm Cameron," though I feared it would come out, "Holy hell, you're hot." I drew a breath to calm myself down, and he edged still closer.

"Look, I get it. You're the good girl to their bad. Every group's got one, and now they're trying to force you over to the dark side. One night, right?" His gaze raked over me, no hint of subtlety, and though a part of me wanted to tell him to take those roaming eyes elsewhere, another part was curious. "And I bet you're tempted," he said, reading my thoughts. "I bet you told yourself you needed this, and you'd be right. You do."

"What do you know about me? With your UT hat and starched shirt. I mean, who the hell dresses like that?"

He laughed, the sound so damn sexy my insides screamed for me to shut up and go along with whatever he had to say. "Not a Tennessee fan, huh?" He cocked his head. "Let me guess—Georgia girl goes to NYU to prove she's bigger than her small town?"

I swallowed hard, my insides boiling at his suggestion—and at how very close he was. Switch out Alabama for Georgia and he'd have pegged me perfectly. Somehow, being read so easily made me want to get away from him. Fast. "Think whatever you like. I should get back to my friends." But when I turned, both Lauren and Grace were out in the bar, talking it up with different guys, well on their way to winning the final task.

"Looks like the bad girls are going to win this round."

My stomach tightened as I peered back over at him. How could someone so hot be so infuriating? "Listen, I don't really need or want your opinion."

"Perhaps. But I'm guessing you could use my lips right about now." He nodded toward the back of the bar, where Lauren sat beside a tall guy with dark hair, her hand on his chest, readying for the kiss. She leaned toward him, just as UT Guy flipped around his baseball cap. "Ready whenever you are, good girl."

I spun back to tell him he could take his lips elsewhere, but then my eyes found his, all wicked fire and sex, his legs slightly open, room for me to step between them. He took my hand and tugged me closer. "Don't think. Just do." And then his mouth found mine, first soft and warm, testing the feel of my lips, the way we moved together. But then the alcohol in my veins seemed to spike, attraction taking over, and I parted my lips, inviting him in, our tongues tangling as he secured me to him. Warmth spread all through me, pooling lower and lower until I felt sure I would lose myself right there in his arms. I'd never been kissed like this, like nothing else mattered, like time stood still. I didn't want it to end.

Finally, I pulled away, unsure of what expression I'd find on his face, and was pleased to see the same heat in his eyes that I felt in my chest. My thoughts jumbled together, rational thinking giving way to temptation. Four years with the same guy, just to watch him leave. Then date after date, all trying to find a spark. Something, anything, only to end up alone. My entire life, I thought I would leave college and move in with my boyfriend, then later get married. But no, I was alone. Well, I didn't want to *be* alone.

Maybe for one night, I didn't have to be.

Biting my lip, I leaned into him, allowing my attraction to him to replace reason, and pressed my lips to his, testing the kiss again, unsure of where this was going. And for once, I didn't care.

Chapter Two

My phone rang from my nightstand, interrupting what had to be the best dream of my life. I scrambled to shut off the loud-pitch sound that drove the knife working through my brain still deeper. Ugh…how much did I drink?

"Hello?" I asked foggily.

"Cammie? Are you sick? Why does it sound like you just woke up?"

I closed my eyes, drawing a long, patience-filled breath, and then opened my mouth to say hello to my mom, when instead a deep voice from beside me said, "Good morning."

"Ah!" I scrambled out of bed, wearing nothing but a white tank top and barely-there panties, and spun around, my eyes locked on the person in my bed. Memories popped into my head from the night before. Lauren and Grace. The game. The karaoke. The girl kissing me. The UT guy.

Holy shit, the UT guy.

My cheeks warmed at the memory of his lips on mine,

on my cheek, my neck, my hand reaching out in invitation as I asked him to come home with me.

Holy shit, I asked him to come home with me.

And unless that dream had manifested into reality or my brain finally had enough and decided to go crazy, here he was. In my bed. Which meant we must have…

"Mom, I've gotta call you back." I hung up the phone, and it immediately rang back. Then when she realized I wasn't answering, the phone *ping*ed with text after text, each one in all caps, screaming for me to call her back RIGHT THIS SECOND. "Dammit." I quickly typed out that there was a spider in my room, my eyes still on the man in my bed.

"You."

"Me." He grinned up at me, bare chest exposed, my white duvet the only thing covering his lower half. Without his UT hat on, he appeared older than me by a few years—maybe late twenties—and oddly familiar. I tried to remember where I might have met him, but in a city of millions, it could have been anywhere or anytime. Or maybe I'd only seen him on the subway or something. I didn't know.

"What are you doing here?"

His mouth quirked as he raised his eyebrows as if to say *shouldn't that be obvious?*

"I don't do this."

"Clearly."

"What's that supposed to mean?"

He stretched his arms out behind him, showing off his defined biceps, then pushed out of the bed, causing my heart to jump into my throat, until I realized he wasn't completely naked. A pair of black boxer briefs covered his ass like they were made just for him. I scowled as I took in his perfectly mussed hair and perfect broad shoulders and unnaturally cut abs. Real people didn't *look* like this guy. Real people were scarred and freckled and flawed. And those flaws were part of what made them beautiful. I preferred guys with just the right mix of flaws. Guys with wrinkled clothes, who wore glasses and—

My random thoughts stopped short as UT Guy slipped on his jeans, then reached for his jacket and pulled out a pair of black frames. "I had to toss my contacts last night, so it's this or I'll need you to walk me home." He flashed me a grin, then fixed his glasses in place, and my cell phone fell from my grasp, bouncing once before landing facedown, clearly ashamed of my ogling.

"Glasses?" I wasn't sure what surprised me more—the glasses or how comfortable he seemed with them on.

He pulled on his shirt and peered over at me. "Yet another reason for that glare of yours? You know, you weren't nearly so mean last night."

Last night. My gaze dropped, embarrassment working through me despite my effort to keep it in check. No, I guess he wouldn't think I was mean last night. I had all but thrown myself at him after that first kiss, desperate for another, and then after an hour of talking and flirting and kissing, I didn't want the night to end, so I'd invited him home with me. Something I had never once done before.

"I'm not a serial killer or something, if that's what has you worried."

"Funny."

He grinned. "I thought so." He took a step toward me and I matched it back, causing him to stop. "Why don't we grab coffee? I can give you a rundown of my résumé. Prove

I'm worthy of your time."

I crossed my arms and stared at him. I'd seen plenty of guys come and go in Lauren's room, and none of them talked about résumés and proving their worth. The glasses might have given me pause, but I was seeing clearly now, and it was time for this embarrassment to end before I fell for his charm and wound up getting burned. "Actually, I have a lot to do today, so if you could just…" I motioned to the door. How exactly did one end a one-night stand? I mean, shouldn't he leave without all this conversation?

He opened his mouth to say more, then cocked his head, taking me in, and closed it back. "It was nice meeting you, Cameron. I wouldn't be sorry if I ran into you again sometime."

Neither would I, I thought, but then immediately pushed that to the back of my mind. I needed this lapse in judgment out of my apartment, so I could focus on readying myself for Monday morning.

"Thanks for…" I waved my hand at the bed, my face burning so bright it could light all of New York. "That."

He bit his lip, fighting another smile. "Maybe you could give me your number, see if you'd like me better if we started at hello." He studied me, and though a part of me was tempted, this wasn't the kind of relationship I wanted. I liked a guy to earn the naked part. This guy had already passed go, won the game, so what would be the point of starting over? At my hesitation, he nodded. "All right, then, I'll just head on. Hope to see you around, Cameron." My body buzzed at the way he said my name, at the reminder of him whispering it against my neck last night. Dear God, it was going to take me days to recover from this. Weeks.

As soon as the door closed behind him, I slumped down on my bed and lay back, brief memories of deep laughter and coy smiles and warm kisses against my cheek. The night might have been reckless, but a part of it was also nice. If only we'd met on different terms, in a different place, a different time, I might have gone to coffee with him. But now I'd end up sitting across from him, picturing him while I wondered if he was picturing me, which would lead to more embarrassment. And I'd had my fix, thanks.

Oh well, it didn't matter. I'd never see him again.

Chapter Three

When Grace called after lunch, suggesting we buy new outfits for our first day, I agreed less because I wanted new clothes and more because I wanted to do something, anything, to get my mind off UT Guy. Hours had passed since he slipped out of my apartment, and yet I still couldn't get him out of my mind. The way his glasses contrasted so sharply with the perfect lines of his face, detracting from his looks yet somehow adding to them all at the same time. And how he didn't seem to care in the least.

"How about this?"

I tiptoed out of my fitting room to find Lauren in front of the three-way mirror, wearing a classy black pencil skirt that hit at her calves and a white blouse tucked into it.

Grace stepped out of her fitting room, just as I was preparing to say *nice but maybe not you* to Lauren, and instead blurted, "You look like a restaurant hostess. No. No, no, no."

Other ladies in the fitting room all peered over then,

curious if she was right, and sadly, Grace was almost always right. Whether or not it was appropriate for her to state her rightness? Entirely different topic.

"What do you think, Cammie?" Lauren's gaze hit mine, a hint of pleading in her eyes. "I'm a buyer. Well, junior buyer. I need to look the part."

Releasing a breath, I walked over to her and scanned the outfit. Now that Grace had said the word "hostess" that was all I could see. "You look amazing in anything, including this. It's just not really you. Let me think." I cocked my head, searching for some trendy addition that would make the outfit work, but who was I kidding? Fashion wasn't my thing.

"Um, a belt, maybe?" I asked, causing Grace to toss her hands and sigh loudly.

"Stay there. I'm going to save you both from yourselves."

She disappeared out of the fitting room and Lauren turned to me. "So, are we going to talk about this morning?"

Lauren had a morning hair appointment, so she didn't have a chance to grill me on UT Guy, though she knew he'd come back to our place. And while I wanted to talk to my friends about him, I didn't know what to say. I wondered how I would have felt if I'd given him my number. Would I hope for a call right now? I would. And though I knew I'd made the right decision, I couldn't help wishing I'd chosen the other path. Exchanged numbers, left the door open for more.

The morning was riddled with all the embarrassment of a classic morning after—messy hair, makeup-streaked face, and awkward conversation. The sun had a way of revealing all the things night hid so beautifully. Yet still…when he turned around and put on his glasses, for a moment I thought it could all work out. My brain did that little fantasy where it worked through the perfect scenario—maybe he was supersmart and had some cool, technical job. Maybe he never hooked up either and somehow we'd fallen into each other's paths. But that was the romantic Cameron talking, the one who found herself watching her mother and stepdad laugh and wishing she could laugh with someone like that.

Sensible Cameron knew better.

"What's there to talk about? I made a mistake."

"He didn't look like a mistake. He looked hot."

"I know. It's just I've never done this before, and I don't want to be one of those girls, ya know?"

Lauren jerked back, her hands on her hips. "Hey. I'm one of those girls."

"I don't mean it like that. I just like structure. I like to know the person I'm in bed with. I like—"

"Commitment."

The word hit me square in the chest, bringing me back to how close I'd been to having it all. Serious boyfriend, degree from NYU, and career well on its way, and then he destroyed me with one blow. And what made it all that much worse, Blaine wasn't a jerk about it. He didn't cheat on me or dump me via text. He just didn't love me.

And somehow that pill was harder to swallow than any of the other scenarios. If he'd cheated, I could lean on my hate, rally with my girls, and have an excuse to hook up with random guys. But he didn't. He kissed my cheek and said goodbye, leaving me with all those feelings of inadequacy. I never realized how badly I wanted a life partner until I no longer had one.

"It doesn't have to be one or the other, Cammie." Lauren

reached for my hand. "You're a good person. Having fun doesn't make you less of a good person."

"You're right. Besides, you hook up all the time and you're still a good person."

"Ha. Ha. But seriously, was it fun? What was his name, anyway?"

I smiled up at her, knowing what she would say to my next statement even before I said the words. "I have no idea."

Lauren laughed, clapping her hands together. This was just the kind of thing Lauren wanted for me and had begged of me for years now. Go wild, forget everything else. "Sorry," she said, after far too much joy at my misery.

"No, you're not."

"Okay, I'm not. But you needed this. Whether you can see it or not, you needed it."

"No, what you need is this." Grace pushed two dresses into my arms. "Trust me. Don't look at the tags or you'll never try them on."

I started immediately for one of the tags, and Grace swatted my hand. "Try them on."

"Fine."

I gave Lauren a fleeting look before stepping back into my fitting room and slipping on the first dress. It was a black button-down sweaterdress. Long-sleeve, knee-length, and sure enough, forever-right Grace was right. The dress was perfect. Absolutely perfect.

Straightening my back, I rose on my toes, appreciating the look once in heels. It was professional, yet trendy. Picturing myself walking into Sanderson-Lowe in this dress, I felt a sense of confidence and pride. But then my gaze dropped to the tag, swaying in the mirror, and I craned my neck to read the price, only to storm out of the fitting room. Grace and Lauren were in front of the mirror with new outfits on.

"Twelve hundred dollars. Are you crazy? I mean, what is it made with, gold stitching or something?"

Grace shook her head. "What? It's a Derek Lam. And it's not *that* much." She picked at one of her manicured nails. "But maybe don't try on the other dress."

"Why? How much is it—two thousand?"

Grace smiled sweetly. "Um, more like four." She swept in behind me before I could faint over four thousand dollars. For a dress. And placed me squarely in front of the mirror. "But look at you. It's so, so perfect, Cammie. Can't you just splurge? Just once? Your inheritance from your dad is plenty to—"

"No. I don't touch that money. You know that."

Guilt crossed her face. "I'm sorry. I didn't mean to bring it up. Really, I'm sorry. But I still think you deserve to have something amazing."

The problem was, she didn't get it. Lauren understood. Like me, she paid for everything, but Grace had never wanted for anything in her life. And I knew deep down she didn't understand why I refused to touch my dad's money. Receiving money for someone dying felt a little like karma trying to buy you off. *Here's some cash for your trouble.* I hated having it, hated receiving statements in the mail, hated the idea that something was left to me after he died, when all I wanted was to have him back.

Pushing aside the pain that always came at the thought of my dad, I lifted my gaze to the mirror to find Grace watching me, hesitant. "I appreciate what you're trying to do. But I can't spend twelve hundred on a dress. I just can't. Can we find something in the two hundred range?"

Lauren nodded to Grace, who looked like I'd just asked her to find me a dress at Target—which, honestly, would be a better option for me—but then she smoothed out her horror and left the fitting room, mumbling to herself as she went.

"She's just trying to help," Lauren said once she was gone. "And she's never had to care about money. She doesn't do it on purpose."

"I know." I glanced in the mirror again. "And it's a fantastic dress. Just twelve hundred dollars? That's not me."

She ran her hands down her own dress, avoiding looking at me. "Kind of like last night."

"You mean UT Guy."

"UT Guy?"

"He was wearing a UT hat."

"Ah. Do you know anything about him? Where he works? Last name? Anything?"

I pulled my hair back into a ponytail. "Yeah, because I didn't catch his first name, but somehow the last name stuck?"

"Good point."

"I have no idea. For all I know, he doesn't have a job, just floats from bar to bar, tempting girls with his perfect hair and glasses."

She grinned. "Glasses?"

"Don't ask." I studied the dress in the mirror, my nerves getting the better of me. "I can't believe we start our jobs tomorrow."

"I know. Ready or not, world, here we come!"

Chapter Four

Standing on the subway platform on a Monday morning in the city was a little like preparing for the start of a race. The yellow line stretched out, telling us to stand behind it, to be courteous and wait our turns, but as soon as the silver train appeared, we all crowded the line, eager to make it on before the car filled up and we had no choice but to miss the train and risk being late. Which wasn't an option. Not today.

The train appeared and the doors opened, but I was a pro now and made my way inside, standing close to a pole and out of the way, then began running through the people at work I'd see today, seeing faces and trying (and often failing) to remember their names.

I knew from the moment I chose NYU that I wanted to work in advertising, and there was no advertising firm better than Sanderson-Lowe. A part of me still couldn't believe they'd hired me.

I pushed off the subway, eager to get to the office. I'd

been this way my entire life. Most saw something new as stressful, dreading and delaying it as long as possible. Lauren had spent all morning in that very mood—talking too fast and switching clothes and generally acting like a crazy version of herself.

But for me, new gave way to possibility. Plus, I was too much of a planner to ever go in unprepared, which was why I'd spent most of the night on my laptop, researching for my morning meeting. My boss, Gayle Litchen, had landed a new client. A power drink company named Blast Water, and the meeting would be to discuss campaign ideas. So far I had five that could work, but I was torn between jumping in or getting acclimated first. Initial appearances were everything in business, and I didn't want to come across as too strong or too meek. There had to be a balance.

I reached Sanderson-Lowe's building, excitement growing in my chest. So what if I was just an account manager. Soon, I would prove my worth and move up the ranks.

Slipping through the revolving door, my eyes scanned the main level—the ivory marble floors and ornate area rugs and mahogany wooden benches. It was a beautiful building. The Starbucks, just inside and to the left, already had an impressive line, and I made a note to arrive early on paydays so I could grab my favorite vanilla latte. I couldn't afford Starbucks every day, but once every two weeks seemed fair enough.

My phone read eight fifteen as I stepped into the elevator. I wanted to be seated at the meeting by eight twenty-five, which just gave me enough time to grab coffee upstairs, put down my things at my cube, and make it to the meeting, where I decided to listen with my mouth shut, smiling and nodding along appropriately. Then after a few days of this, I'd strike. They'd be wowed and my career would soar from there. All right, maybe a stretch, but a girl could hope.

The thought made me smile, but then the doors to the elevator closed, and my chest tightened as I began to sing silently. *Mary had a little lamb, little lamb, little lamb...* I continued my silent song, fighting the urge to close my eyes, to suck in a sharp breath, to panic. The space closed in all around me, the elevator packed with people. If this elevator got stuck, I'd—

No.

Dipping my head, I resumed my song, telling myself to breathe easily, to sing and forget. I sang whatever nursery rhyme first came to mind the moment I stepped foot into an elevator, all so I could handle the doors closing, the delay before it moved, the panic that rose in my chest when I realized I was on a slow elevator instead of the fast ones I preferred.

I knew the very moment I'd become so claustrophobic. It was just after my dad died, and I kept feeling like the walls were closing in all around me. I couldn't breathe in my room. Couldn't breathe in the bathroom. The outdoors became my refuge, the open air around me, nothing closing in. Eventually, it became easier to handle, and now the only issues I had were elevators and airplanes, and I had coping mechanisms with both. Nursery rhymes on elevators and heavy antianxiety pills when I flew. It wasn't a perfect system, but it worked for me.

The elevator rose to the second floor, third, fourth, and then finally I drew a breath and released it slowly as the doors slid open to the fifth floor. I stepped off the elevator like it was no big deal, even though my heart raced and my palms were clammy. *Inhale, exhale. Inhale, exhale. Everything was fine.*

I relaxed more with each step and peered around, remembering the first time I visited the Sanderson-Lowe floor. The reception area of Sanderson-Lowe was modern in every way—bright yellow triangular chairs, abstract paintings. When I toured the office on my second interview, they pointed out the lounge room—complete with Ping-Pong table and widescreen TV—the nap room, the soundproof thinking room. I had interviewed with five different agencies, but none of them seemed to care as much about quality of life as Sanderson-Lowe. Or maybe it was just that they expected us to live at the office.

The receptionist, a redhead around my age, smiled wide when she saw me. She had long, slender limbs, high cheekbones, shiny, perfectly styled hair. She reminded me of Grace in that put-together way only money could buy.

"Hi, I'm Cameron Lawson. A new account manager." I tried not to grin as I said the title, but failed miserably. I was employed, a real adult. I could hardly contain myself. Dad would be so proud.

"Welcome to Sanderson-Lowe," she said, her voice kind. "I'm Alexa. You can meet the others in conference room 1A, just down the hall there." She pointed to her left, and I paused, staring down the long hallway, my nerves kicking up. Should I speak in the meeting or keep quiet? Should I bring in a notepad and pen or just my phone? Did people still use notepads and pens when there were things like smartphones and iPads?

Alexa smiled like she could read my thoughts. "Why

don't you grab coffee first? It helps to go in carrying something. The lounge is through there." She motioned to her right this time, and I nodded appreciatively.

"Thanks, it's just a little…intimidating."

"Oh, I know. I've been here for five months and I still get nervous every time Aidan Truitt walks by."

Aidan Truitt—aka the chief creative director. He was Gayle's boss, so I'd assumed I'd have little interaction with him. Now I felt my nervousness spiking again. I'd researched Sanderson-Lowe and then Gayle before my interview, knowing she would be my boss should they offer me the job. It never occurred to me to research others in the company, but maybe I should have prepared better. Checked out the top-tier executives and everyone in her division, only I didn't really know my division yet and—

"Are you okay?" Alexa asked. I didn't realize that I was staring at the lounge door, likely with a look of horror on my face. "Don't worry, I'll go in with you." She stepped around her desk and pushed through the door, holding it open for me to slip inside.

There was no one else in there, so I took the opportunity to question Alexa on my new boss—well, my boss's boss. "Yeah, I didn't get to meet him when I interviewed. Is he scary?"

Immediately she spun around, a to-go coffee cup with Sanderson-Lowe's logo printed on it in hand. "You haven't met Aidan?"

I shook my head as I took the cup and began making my coffee. "No. Though Gayle made him sound intense."

"Yeah, intensely hot."

I did a double take. "He's *what*?" Did she say hot? I

pictured an older man, graying, with a slight hunch. Then again, maybe Alexa was into sixty-year-olds with back problems.

She peered over at the closed door and then leaned in closer. "You have no idea. Rumor has it he's the reason for the no-fraternizing policy."

"No fraternizing…you mean he's…?"

"Not *is,* presently, but yeah, certainly *did*. A lot. That's why there's been such turnover. They couldn't get a female on staff below the age of thirty to stay away from him, so the partners issued a strict no-fraternizing policy, and Aidan hasn't touched a Sanderson-Lowe employee since. Not that I could blame the girls."

Just then Gayle walked in, and I had to fight to rein in my crazy beating heart. The last thing I wanted was for Gayle to hear us talking about Aidan like that. "Good, Cameron, I was looking for you. Are you ready? The meeting's about to begin, and I wanted to introduce you to the staff before it gets started."

"Of course," I said, a little too loudly, but Gayle was already leaving the lounge, me following quickly behind her.

I peeked through the glass to the group already seated around the long rectangular table. There was a mix of men and women; each dressed so differently it was impossible to know what was appropriate. Hell, one guy was even wearing a T-shirt. Gayle stood behind a pair of open chairs, and suddenly all eyes were on me. "Everyone, this is Cameron Lawson, our newest account manager. She'll be assisting on all my accounts."

We sat down and one by one the people around the table introduced themselves. I tried to follow their names, but I'd always been a faces person, the names disappearing into the cracks of my memory.

I reached across for a notepad and pen in the middle of the table, and a man sitting just in front of it—Brody?— pushed the stack my way to make it easier for me to grab. "Thanks," I said, smiling.

"You're welcome."

The table sectioned out into different conversations. The men discussed the game from the night before. (I had no idea which game they meant.) The ladies at the opposite side from Gayle and me were talking about some preservative that caused cancer. I opened my mouth to say that everything but bananas and water seemed to cause cancer these days, but closed it back, sure I'd sound like a know-it-all, which wasn't a stretch of the truth. Still, today was an observation day. Learn the team, pay attention, try not to piss anyone off.

Gayle turned to me then, clearly sensing my unease. "They're all nice. Don't worry."

"They seem great."

"And Aidan is brilliant. You'll learn a lot from him."

"I didn't think I would actually work with him much." Dammit. Why didn't I research Aidan Truitt?

"You won't really, but he likes to be very involved with our team. He leads all the meetings. Likes to have a hand in everything. Some say he micromanages, but I think he just wants us to know that we're not in the thick of it alone. Plus, he's really young for the job and I think a part of him misses the creative side." Her gaze shifted to the door. "And speaking of…"

I turned just as the door opened. A man stood inside the doorframe, his head facing away from us as he said something to Alexa. He wore an impeccably tailored navy suit, his dirty-blond hair styled back with a hint of gel. I could see why Alexa said he was hot, even from behind. She nodded to him, then he stepped into the room, and suddenly my world turned on its axis, like I'd entered some alternate reality.

My heart jumped into my throat, my pulse speeding up as my stomach flipped. A memory hit of warm breath on my neck, and I jolted back, my hand colliding with my coffee cup and sending its contents across the table. "Shit." I leaped up at the same time as everyone else, one of the guys grabbing a pack of paper towels and blotting the mess. The women smiled encouragingly at me like they'd all been here before. But they had no freaking idea.

And that's when his gaze landed on me. He froze just as he was setting down his iPad, his eyes wide, his mouth slack. Another traitorous memory slipped through, that mouth on mine, his teeth biting my bottom lip just before his tongue—

"You."

I drew a breath, ignoring my shaky hands and wobbly knees. "Me."

Gayle was at my side in a second. "I'm sorry," she said in an attempt to save me. "It's Cameron's first day. I'm sure she's a little nervous."

If only that were the problem.

Collecting himself, he straightened, licking his lips once, his eyes on me. "Easy mistake. Could happen to anyone." He grinned, a hint of amusement crossing his face at the double meaning. My teeth ground together as I fought to rein in my emotions.

"Well, introduce me to our newest team member," he

said to Gayle.

Gayle smiled at me. "This is Cameron Lawson, our newest account manager. She will be helping on all my accounts, including Blast, which was why I requested she attend our meeting today. Cameron, meet Aidan Truitt. Our chief creative director."

I lifted my eyes to his, my heart now wallowing on the ground, never to emerge again. Aidan Truitt. My boss. My *boss's* boss.

Aka—UT Guy.

Chapter Five

"Welcome to the team, Cameron." He held out his hand for me to shake, and I started to place mine in his, though every part of me wanted to back away, to disappear—to run. But this was adulthood. No running allowed.

I placed my hand in his, our eyes locked, and for a moment, we were back there. At the bar, laughing, fingers interlaced, electricity moving between us. The man before me wasn't UT Guy, yet somewhere in his gaze I saw the guy I'd met, felt the spark, understood why he'd made it back to my apartment.

My father used to say only a few people would ever fully connect with you. See you for who you are and stay there anyway. He said you knew it when you met them, felt the change in the air, the calm in your belly. The person could be a friend, a relative—a lover. But forever, that person would be a match. Years could pass and conversation would still feel easy, like no time had passed at all.

Since I was little, I would watch for these people. Listen to their voices, hear their stories, look into their eyes. And yet after thousands of occurrences and introductions, I'd felt that match with only two people—my stepdad, Eric, which always made me feel a tiny bit guilty, and Lauren. I loved Grace, but Grace was an acquired taste, like beer or wine or coffee. You grew to appreciate her the more time you spent around her, but our connection wasn't instantaneous. Not like Eric. Or Lauren.

Or Aidan.

The realization that I'd met a third connection and that he was my boss was enough to unnerve me even more than the fact that we'd hooked up. Sex complicated things, but this was different—more.

I smiled a little at the memory of our time at the bar, the easy conversation, and he smiled back, the expression soft, before we remembered that all eyes were on us, and he cleared his throat and took the seat at the end of the table. The seat directly beside me. Clearly the gods viewed this day as one of the great tests of my lifetime. *Here you go, Cammie, survive this and you'll earn a random act of kindness. Congratulations!*

Taking my seat, I concentrated on the notepad in front of me, jotting down today's date in the top right corner like I always did. Somehow I still preferred to take notes on paper, like the page pulled out my thoughts better than one of my devices. I set my pen down beside the notepad, vertical as always, and accidentally marked the page. It took every ounce of my control not to flip the sheet and begin again.

Aidan settled in his seat, and then as though someone flipped a switch, he was all business, not at all the same carefree man from the bar. He eyed each of us. "Okay, where are we? Gayle, go." It was as though he had two personalities. Or maybe I'd just been that drunk.

"Right," she said, launching into the details of the campaign while the rest of us took notes, some on the notepads, others in their phones or iPads. Aidan simply listened, but something in the way his eyes had transformed from that hint of humor before to complete seriousness now told me he was retaining and processing more than the rest of us ever could.

Blast Water wanted a campaign focused on college football, in an effort to sway some of the teams from Gatorade. They wanted to speak to the fans of the schools, push that their product could help teams succeed. In short, there couldn't be a better campaign for me to work on. I knew college football. I'd been around it my whole life.

"Okay," Aidan said after Gayle had finished. "Am I safe in assuming that everyone in this room has attended a college football game?" The table went quiet.

He placed his elbows on the table and locked his hands together in front of him. "Seriously?"

"I have," Brody said. "I went to Notre Dame. There's no program like Notre Dame's."

I rolled my eyes before I could stop myself. "Right."

Aidan's gaze snapped over to me. "Did you want to add something, Cameron?"

I focused on the table. God. *Keep your mouth shut, Cameron.* There was no reason to get into this. Let the fight go. And then before I could help it, my know-it-all mouth was speaking too fast for my brain to keep up. "Nothing. It's just Alabama would crush them. In fact, most SEC schools would crush them."

I folded my hands in front of me, completely mortified at my outburst, but I couldn't help it. Though I'd chosen NYU, my roots were still in Birmingham, where I grew up, and as loyal as ever to the University of Alabama, where my parents went to college. My gaze drifted up to Aidan, curious if he would agree with me. After all, UT was also in the SEC, but he didn't meet my stare.

Instead, amusement spread across his face again, and I wondered if he viewed me as some circus act. *Check out the new entertainment for Sanderson-Lowe.* He glanced over at Brody, who was clearly fuming, but refused to argue with me in front of Aidan. "Okay, then. So we have a few who know the game. Great. Now, think about the rush of the first home game. The intensity of the crowd. The excitement on the field. How can we convey that in a short thirty- or sixty-second ad?"

Everyone spoke at once, throwing out ideas and arguing and generally making no sense at all. I wondered if every meeting ran this way. Finally Aidan's gaze fell back on me, the new kid, and I knew I was about to be placed on the spot.

"What about you?"

My eyes shot to Gayle and she nodded reassuringly. "Well," I said, "I was thinking we should focus on an IMC approach, which takes a look at the whole marketing picture instead of a single piece. I.e. television. I was thinking—" Laughter erupted around the table before I could continue. "What?" I asked, my voice much smaller than before.

Brody opened his mouth, but it was Aidan who spoke. "This isn't a classroom. I don't want a textbook definition of what's good. I want originality. I want inspiration. Your job isn't to recite to me what you learned over the last four

years. It's to use your brain to come up with something new."
He turned away from me and never glanced my way again.
His voice wasn't hateful, but there was no care in his words.
Straight and to the point—exactly how he should treat any-
one else in that room.

So why did I feel like he should treat me differently? He
shouldn't, couldn't. That would be the definition of inappropriate. Regardless of what happened between us, Aidan ran
my division. He was just doing his job. Unlike me.

I wanted to sink into my chair. Originality. Right. My
first meeting at my first job, and I had failed.

• • •

I didn't speak again for the rest of the meeting. I listened, I
observed, but I never spoke, wishing I had just kept to my
original plan. Gayle came over to me once it was over. "Don't
let them rattle you. Everyone shoots off textbook definitions
on their first day. It's all we know. Aidan just…" She shook
her head, her gaze locking on Aidan's office across the room.
He was already inside, walking around, his cell to his ear.
The wall facing us was all glass, even the door. His title and
name were etched into the door, visible only if you stood
right in front of it. He had blinds ready to close off the rest of
us from his world, but Gayle said he rarely used them.

"Aidan's hard," she continued, her tone kind. "But it's
because he's good. He just wants you to be that good, too.
Shake it off, okay? I have some calls to make. Think you
could do some research for me?" She passed me a list, all
pertaining to Blast and Gatorade. I nodded to her, and she
showed me to my cube before setting off for her office.

I started up my email so I would see if Gayle sent something my way, and immediately locked in on an email in my in-box. But it wasn't from Gayle—it was from Aidan.

Clicking the email, I cycled through possible scenarios. I hated the unknown. I had to work out every side of a situation, so I would know how to handle it. So I could avoid failure. Getting hired at Sanderson-Lowe had proved to me that all my hard work had paid off. And now, in one drunken moment of weakness, it could all slip away.

My attention fell on the email, my heart speeding up as I read the words:

Can you come to my office please?

And there it was, the big *I'm sorry, you're fired.* Or *you'll have to transfer to a different department.* But surely he couldn't fire me. We hadn't known. Just like he'd said, it could happen to anyone. And I didn't want to move to a different department. I adored Gayle already and knew she and I would work well together. One mistake shouldn't change anything.

I wouldn't let it.

Our floor sat quiet except for the clicking of computer keys and the occasional phone conversation, making the walk to Aidan's office feel almost painful. A nice older lady smiled up at me from the desk outside his office.

"Can I help you?"

"Yes, I'm here to see A—Mr. Truitt."

"Of course." She reached for her phone to let him know, just as he glanced up from his desk and called for me to come on in.

Closing the door behind me, I glanced around, trying to reconcile UT Guy with Aidan. There was a University of Tennessee diploma on the right-hand wall, and just below it an MBA from Columbia. Most would put the advanced degree above the undergrad, especially considering it was Ivy League, but then something told me Aidan wasn't like most people.

"Have a seat," he said.

I sat in one of the yellow chairs in front of his desk. Clearly, whoever decorated Sanderson-Lowe's floor had a thing for yellow.

Aidan leaned forward, his forearms resting on his desk, and as I looked up and into his eyes I wondered if I would have kissed this version of him. Would I have laughed like I did? Would I have asked him back to my apartment? Likely not.

He seemed to read my mind. "I like to relax when I'm not here, shake off the business week. So you'll usually find me in jeans and that UT hat. I've had it for years and I…" He trailed off. "Sorry. Anyway, I'm sure you realize how complicated this is?"

I nodded.

"I asked for your number before, but that's not really appropriate now." He grinned, the smile almost boyish. God, he was handsome. Not just hot or sexy. He was handsome. Rough, yet polished. It was a beautiful combination.

"Right…" My turn to trail off.

"As a rule, I don't date women at the office." He laughed. "Actually, I don't date at all."

My eyes flashed up, anger sparking inside me. *Let it go. Just let it go.* But I was never one to let anything go. "A little presumptuous, don't you think? I never asked you for a date.

I never asked for your number. And I didn't offer you mine."

He smiled again, a real, full smile, and for a second, my anger slipped, my heartbeat speeding up. I wasn't sure if he was laughing at me or not, but I wanted to tell him to put that weapon away if he wanted me to get any work done. Silence grew between us, tension and attraction igniting. My body warmed under his stare, and I wondered if he was thinking about Saturday night, if it had been as good for him as it had been for me. Then cursing myself for even thinking about it, I pushed to standing.

"So, was that all?" I asked, eager to get out of there so I could breathe again.

Aidan considered me. "Yes."

"Good. Then while we're discussing appropriate, I'd like to make a few requests."

"I'm listening."

I squared my shoulders and lifted my chin. "None of those half-laughing smiles." The corners of his mouth twitched, and I pointed at him. "See, that. That right there. None of those."

With obvious effort, he relaxed his face. "All right. Anything else?"

I stared back at him, watching as his eyes traveled over me quickly before returning to my face, like he couldn't control himself. Fresh rage burned in my chest. Damn if I was going to come to work every day and stand here while he imagined all my parts. "Just one." Drawing a breath, I leaned over his desk, inches from his face, "No picturing me naked. Not even a little. To you, I'm forever clothed. Got it?" Then I turned and bolted out of his office, sure I could hear his laughter long after the door closed behind me.

Chapter Six

Lunch consisted of a dry turkey sandwich from downstairs at my desk so I could continue my research for Gayle, and before long the office had grown quiet, the day coming to a close. I quickly texted Lauren to meet me at the Irish pub just down from my office, knowing she wouldn't be able to refuse.

Stuffing my phone back into my bag, I peeked slowly over the top of my cube, hoping Aidan had gone home for the day, but his office was lit. He sat at his desk, focused on his Mac, working away as though it were midday instead of night.

I tried not to watch him as he worked. The way his hair fell into his eyes after a while and how he left it that way for several seconds before sweeping it out of his face. Like he was too focused on what he was doing to care. He sat in perfect posture, and every few minutes he would stare at the wall across from him before diving back into whatever he worked on. I wondered what was on that wall, if there was a photo there or a painting or maybe his favorite magazine ad. He picked up his phone a few times, but he never took a call, like he wanted to reach out to someone or maybe he hoped the person would reach out to him. And then finally, it was past seven, and I signed off, packed up my laptop, and went for the door. My gaze landed on Aidan again before I left. I couldn't help it. Something about him kept me coming back.

Like always, I chose a different elevator from the one I took this morning, forever hoping to find some superfast elevator that traveled at near light speed. So far no luck. I drew a long breath and stepped into my choice, my eyes widening as the doors closed, and then I hummed "Baa, Baa, Black Sheep" until the doors popped back open and my breathing returned to normal. I pushed out of the building toward the pub, drawing in the night air as soon as it hit my face. My shoulders were tight and my feet were sore and my brain felt like it already needed a day off.

The Irish pub was smaller than most bars we frequented, with ten or so tables and then the bar. The Giants were on the wide-screen, and besides me, there was only a handful of people there. I imagined within an hour it would be packed, but for now, it was nice.

Securing a table away from the door, I laid out my notes from the morning meeting and then the research I had found for Gayle. I'd emailed her my findings before I left for the day, but I'd also printed a copy for myself.

"Vodka tonic," I said to the waitress, just as my phone buzzed with a text from Lauren saying she'd be late. I slid my phone back into my bag and dived into the notes. I was reading over Brody's idea of colored water dripping like sweat off the top players in any given division, which had been done, when the door to the bar opened. My gaze lifted, curious if Grace had been able to join us after all, but it wasn't Grace or Lauren.

It was Aidan.

I slumped down in my chair and raised my notes up to hide my face. Why didn't I choose a bar away from the office? I peeked over my notes. He was at the bar in just a few steps, laughing with the bartender, and I thought of how freely he had laughed with me on Saturday night. It was a different look for him. Laughing. A good look.

He ordered something I couldn't hear and turned around to watch the game, when his eyes locked on mine. I ducked back down, praying he hadn't actually seen me, which was maybe my stupidest thought all day, and then I heard the screeching sound of the chair across from me being pulled away from the table.

"Is this seat taken?"

I closed my eyes and dropped my notes at the sound of his voice. "I suppose not. Is there something I can do for you?" My voice held a hint of agitation that I couldn't push away. He might be my boss, but I was still annoyed at his *I don't date* BS. As though I expected a date. As though I *wanted* a date. Like every woman he passed by longed to go out with him, which likely they did, but gah. People didn't admit that crap out loud.

Instead of answering my question, he picked up my notes and turned them around so he could read them. "Hey," I called, before I could stop myself. "Have you ever heard of asking?"

Fantastic, Cameron. Go ahead and get yourself fired on

the first day.

But he only smirked as his gaze dropped to the notes, UT Guy reappearing before me. "Detailed. Good." His eyes lifted, and the intensity in them made my heartbeat kick up. I knew the look had less to do with me and more to do with his passion for the job, but still, why did he have to be so hot? It'd be so much easier if Aidan were the sixty-year-old with back problems I'd envisioned.

Or if I hadn't slept with him.

"Glad you picked up on the redundancy of the sweat idea. You're right, it has been done." He continued through my notes, each second growing more painful. I wondered what his expressions meant, why he nodded at times or his eyebrows threaded together at others. What did he see in my work? In me? I needed another drink to survive this. I needed fifty more drinks.

Finally, he returned my notebook to me and glanced up. "What I'm not seeing here are your ideas."

I hesitated. "That's because my ideas aren't there. I keep them here." I tapped my phone. "I want to be able to find them easily, make changes to them while I'm walking to work or in a cab or on the subway. It's just easier."

He waved to the waitress, who brought over his drink. "Anything else for you, Aidan?"

I did a double take at her using his first name. Clearly, he was a regular.

"No, thanks. Anything for you, Cameron?" I eyed my almost-empty drink and he grinned. "She'll have another."

"It's okay. Really. I can—"

"She'll have another," he repeated to the waitress, who shrugged at me and went on back to the bar.

As soon as she was gone, Aidan leaned in close, his hair falling a bit over his eyes in that impossibly sexy way, and I expected him to launch into a tirade, a lesson, something that would make me feel even worse, when he said, "About today…"

"Yes?" I prepared myself for his epic apology for the no-dating comment. A declaration that he wished he could date me, wished I would have given him my number. That he wouldn't have been able to wait twenty-four hours to call. The whole *You've Got Mail* scene played out right here. It would be sweet, endearing, would make me wish we *could* date, so I could find out which version of him was the real Aidan.

But instead he said, "I'm sorry if I seemed a little rough in the meeting. It's a sink-or-swim business, and they were about to rip you apart. That's how it's done. Which was why it had to come from me. I've made every person in that room feel like an amateur at some point."

I blinked. "Wait, what?"

"The morning meeting? Did you think I was going to say something else?"

"No, I just…no."

He tilted his head, waiting, his lips twitching in their effort to keep from forming a half grin. "I'm listening."

"I said it was nothing."

"Yet, still here waiting."

"Fine. I thought you might apologize for the no-dating thing."

His expression turned playful, and he pushed out of his chair. "Nothing to apologize for there. I *don't* date."

It didn't matter if he dated. It was that he assumed I

wanted a date. I opened my mouth to say as much, when Lauren rushed up to our table, preventing me from going off on him properly. She was rambling about a fashion emergency at work, but I wasn't listening. I was trying to rein in my emotions, or else I'd be searching for a job tomorrow. How could he have been so charming and funny on Saturday night and now be such an ass? And why did I get the feeling the jerk-Aidan wasn't the real him?

"Here, take my seat," he said to Lauren. "I was just leaving."

I wanted to ask him to stay, to see if UT Guy would reappear, see if that connection I'd felt with him would return, but I couldn't. Regardless of the casual persona he took on at the bar, he was my boss.

Our eyes met one last time, and in his I saw a change, if only slight, but it was there. A battle, a feeling, something. But then his gaze dropped, the connection lost, and he disappeared out the door without a backward glance.

Chapter Seven

"Okay. Explain," Lauren said, her face engulfed in one of those *spill it, girl* smiles. She settled into Aidan's chair and waited for me to speak. Her pin-straight hair was fastened back with a bronze peacock clip. Some new thing they'd ordered for Bergdorf's that they were hoping would take off, but likely wouldn't. "So?"

I sighed heavily, stalling. "Geez, take a breath before you fall over."

"Forget breathing, Cammie. UT Guy was just sitting at your table, all in your space. Don't even try to tell me that you're not freaking out right now. And holy wow, up close he's even hotter than I remembered. He's like a dream. God." She glanced back at the door.

"A dream? What are you, fifteen? Did you have a round on the walk over here or something? He isn't a dream. He's—" I shook my head. Who was I kidding? He was totally a dream, but I refused to admit that out loud. "And you have no idea how jacked-up this all became today. UT Guy? Yeah, he's my boss."

Lauren choked on her drink—well, my drink, which she'd taken the liberty of stealing—and began sputtering. "No effing way. UT Guy is your boss? How is that possible? He's like twenty-eight tops, right?"

I filled her in on the full exchange from the morning. Even explaining the horrid situation made my cheeks flame. "It was beyond humiliating."

"So, no banging in his office? I mean you've already gone there, so what's the harm in a little more action?"

I smiled. Leave it to Lauren to make me laugh even after a day like this. "Yeah, no. Sorry to disappoint you. The company has a strict no-fraternizing policy, which according to our admin was created to keep Aidan away from innocent new hires like me."

The wow look on her face told me this was the best piece of information I'd given her yet. "So he isn't against it, then?"

"I don't know, probably all rumors. He said he'd never dated anyone at the office. That he doesn't date at all. Just as well. I'd get fired."

She opened her mouth, then closed it. "Right, and you've been dreaming about this job for four years." We sat in silence for a second, then she smirked. "But I bet he'd totally be worth it."

I shrugged. "Doesn't matter. So tell me about your first day at Bergdorf's as a hot new buyer."

"Junior buyer, and even that seems like a fancy title for what I really do." She launched into coffee runs and sorting files and clothes and doing any and everything other than buying. It's funny how fabulous our jobs sounded to us before we'd actually started them. Now, reality had set in. We were at the bottom of the barrel, scraping away with a salary so low it should be against the law, all in hopes of moving up.

Right now, I planned to starve for lunch the next day to make up for our drinks. You spend four years in college, and never once did they tell you how hard it'd be once you left. How slow and painful the job hunt could be. How the salaries were a joke and the apartments cost a fortune. Sure, some new graduates, like Grace, had trust funds and families willing to support them while their careers took off. But Lauren and I were not part of that club. Lauren was raised on a farm out in Oklahoma, and my family…well, let's just say I'd made it my mission at twelve when my dad died to get the hell out of there. It wasn't that I didn't love my mom and even my stepdad, Eric. I did. But I didn't want to marry at twenty-two and have babies at twenty-five, my life set even before I'd begun living it.

I'd spent the better part of my four years at NYU learning to speak without an accent and begging my parents to come visit me here so they could see this part of my life. See why I loved it. But it always ended in an argument. So I would go home, listen to my aunts rave about my cousins and their husbands and children, all the while feeling less and less like my accomplishments mattered. I loved going home, the amazing food and comfort of our house, but for once, I wanted Mom to pipe up and brag about me. It never happened.

Sadness washed over me at the thought, and then a voice from over my shoulder said, "Can I buy you ladies another round?"

Lauren smiled. "Grace! I thought you couldn't come?"

Grace settled into the third chair and for the rest of the evening I forgot about work and Aidan, glad to have my friends beside me.

Now, if only I could forget about UT Guy.

• • •

I left Lauren and Grace an hour later, eager to get back home so I could sort through my day in private.

As soon as I closed the door to my apartment and tossed my keys in the basket we kept on the kitchen counter, I went immediately to the shower. Showers were one of my least favorite things in the world—the aggravation of shaving and drying hair too much for me to stand—but my shoulders were still tight from the day, and I needed to unwind.

I hit the docking station I kept in my bathroom and surfed through until I found the song I craved—"Tuesday's Gone." My dad, my real dad, was a major classic rock fan, and my mom used to joke that when I'd scream as a baby, he'd play me Lynyrd Skynyrd and I'd quiet down every time. Now I played the band whenever I felt like I was losing myself, my focus, and needed to come back to center. After all, it was my dad who gave me my first set of wings. He was a pilot, and every time he'd return home he'd tell me he wanted me to go places, to see the world, to become the best possible version of myself. To me, he was telling me to leave Alabama and to never look back. And so I did. I just never realized that fulfilling my dad's greatest wishes for me would break my mom's heart so thoroughly.

The memory hit me like it'd happened yesterday. I'd

gotten all my college acceptance letters and had finally made my choice. I still remembered the look on Mom's face when I told her I'd chosen NYU. How she had at first said no, then that we couldn't afford it, then the weather and the crime rate, and then before long, she was crying. I stared at her, lost as to how the happiest moment in my life could make her so miserable. She didn't understand. I couldn't breathe there. I couldn't voice a single opinion without having someone look at me like I'd grown horns. My perfect cousins hated me, and the rest of my family treated me like I was a stranger. After all, I was a hard-core Democrat in a Republican state. A foreigner. My upbringing marked me a Southerner, but I'd never been Southern a day in my life.

I grabbed my navy pajamas from the darks side of my pajama drawer and lay back against my bed, my phone beside me. I had just tucked my legs under the covers and closed my eyes when my phone vibrated with a new email. I clicked the *work* folder, and then nearly dropped my phone as I read the name at the top.

Aidan Truitt.

Sitting up and crossing my legs, my gaze zeroed in on the empty subject line. A thousand things began to run through my mind—was he writing to lecture me? To ask me to do something? To fire me? Why was I so afraid of being fired? Surely that didn't happen on your first day. I didn't know, but as I ran through scenarios, each possibility felt more probable than the last. Finally, I ordered myself to stop being a wuss and hit the damn email. Only seven words and a letter.

My office, 9 a.m. Bring your notes.

- A

Chapter Eight

Lauren was still in bed when I crept out of our apartment at seven thirty the following morning. I had no idea what Aidan wanted with me at nine, but I planned to get to the office before him so I could prepare.

I exited a different elevator from the two I'd taken yesterday—my favorite of the three—to a quiet floor, no Alexa, no Gayle, no one rushing down the halls and no sounds from the cubicles as I passed. I was just about to slide my gym bag under my desk when a deep voice asked, "Are you a before or after work kind of girl?"

My back straightened, and I spun around to see Aidan leaning against my cube. "Excuse me?" I asked.

"The bag. I'm assuming it's for working out?"

"Oh, yeah." So not what I thought he was asking. "I take kickboxing a few days a week at my gym. Keeps my mom happy. The whole self-defense thing."

His eyebrows lifted. "Kickboxing, huh? That's unexpected."

I grinned. "Let me guess. You expected yoga?" I thought of Grace's failed attempt to get me into yoga and laughed. I would try to talk and she'd *shh* me and then a few minutes would pass and I'd try again, only to receive another sharp look. She didn't invite me back. "You don't know me very well."

He took a small step toward me, an inch, no more, but all of a sudden I couldn't breathe. "I know that you're originally from Birmingham and likely moved to New York to prove a point to yourself as much as anyone else. I know you were in the top of your class. That you received three job offers, all from top agencies." Another step. "And I know that the girl from Saturday night who told me all this? The one who relaxed, maybe for the first time in her life? You think that girl isn't you, but she's in there. It's okay to let her out once in a while. To let go." He held my gaze for a second longer, then cleared his throat and started down the hall, toward his office. "I'm ready when you are."

I collapsed into my chair as soon as it was safe, sure that if I didn't sit I would fall. What the hell just happened? His words replayed in my mind, the way his voice had dipped down, and suddenly, every fiber in me longed to let my carefree side go—straight to Aidan's office to see if we could pick up where we'd left off Saturday night. I'd never had such an immediate attraction to a man in my life. A man who just so happened to be my boss. I tried to remind myself of that fact every time these thoughts hit me, but so far the word "boss" was doing little more than making him even hotter.

I clenched my eyes shut, irritated that I was allowing

myself to lose control. And in only two days. I needed to focus on the job, keep my emotions in check—remember how hard I'd worked to get this job.

My computer fired up, and I told myself I was checking my email to be responsible, but really it was to give my brain something productive to do. Something other than think about a certain boss. I couldn't go in there now, the image of his body tangled in my sheets so fresh in my mind.

After a few minutes of stalling, I pushed out of my chair, grabbed my phone and my notes, and started toward his office, refusing to look up. Something told me I would see UT Guy watching me, not Aidan, and I couldn't handle that version of him. Not now.

I knocked lightly on the glass door before slowly opening it. "Aidan?"

"Come in." His voice was low, too low. The sort of voice that made your insides twist and curl and dream about things you had no right dreaming about. I gave him a fleeting look before closing the door and walking over to his desk. He was leaning back in his chair, his hair styled out of his eyes. He'd rolled his sleeves to his elbows, showing off the contours of his forearms. Forearms that had cradled me close just days before.

Ugh. Stop it.

"Deep thought?" The corner of his mouth quirked up just a touch, and instantly, my cheeks burst into flames. Damn skin. I needed medication or something. Like a green pill that would cancel out the red whenever my emotions spiked.

I forced my expression to remain even. "Just wondering why you wanted to see me this morning."

Aidan leaned forward, his eyes locked on mine. "I thought that was obvious."

The warmth in my cheeks spread through me, refusing to be contained. Why did he have to say things like that? Words that to anyone else would mean nothing at all, yet his tone, his expression, everything about him said something more. He was my boss, and in truth, if he were anyone else I would be offended, even worried, but with Aidan…

I sat down in the chair across from him and crossed my legs. "Not to me."

The moment lingered long, tension building, and then he turned his monitor toward me so I could see what was on the screen. It was an ad mock-up from creative, but nothing about it was creative. The colors were too bold, the text too heavy, the images impossible to focus on.

"Did you bring your notes?"

Without thinking, I passed him my notebook and phone, our fingers touching in the exchange, the connection so intense I had to jerk away. Was it suddenly very, very hot in his office?

"Password?"

He started to pass it back to me, when I said, "5267." His eyebrows lifted, and I added, "It was my father's birthday."

"Was?" he asked, his tone hesitant.

"He died in a plane crash when I was twelve. He was the pilot." I had no idea why I admitted that to him. I could have just shrugged, claimed it was a random number, but something about Aidan made me feel too raw to lie. Like with the phone itself—why had I passed it to him so easily? I was standing right there, so it wasn't like he could search my phone, but a person's phone was a sacred thing. Home to friends and family, embarrassing texts and photos that should have been deleted the moment they were snapped. Yet I had passed mine to him without hesitation.

It took me a second to realize that he was watching me. I looked up, unwilling to show too much emotion. My dad died. It was a long time ago, and while I would always feel that ache in my chest, more than anything I just wanted to be the daughter he raised. To make him proud. I expected Aidan to say he was sorry or ask more questions, but he simply nodded, typed in the password, and then began reading the notes I had up on the screen. My ideas for the campaign.

He didn't speak as he read them or nod or give any indication that he had any opinion at all. But then he set my phone down and leaned back in his chair, his hands linked behind his head as he stared past me. I turned around to see what was on the wall behind me, the same wall I'd seen him focused on the night before. It was a painting of a young man with a toy train facing a man who was attempting to pull a locomotive with a rope. I studied the painting for a long time, then glanced back at Aidan to find him watching me.

"It's a Pawel Kuczynski piece."

"It's deep." I eyed the painting again.

"His work is very satirical. A different look at the world. That's what I try to do here. I want our ads to be different, to take a different approach to advertising. It isn't enough to catch the consumer's attention. You have to make them never forget."

The passion in his voice made me want to sit and talk to him for hours about work, to pick apart his brain and discover how he'd risen in the company in such a short amount of time, but I knew I shouldn't. Aidan had already made an impact on me.

I focused back on our campaign. "Is that what you're trying for there?" I asked, pointing at his screen. The ad was horrible, but maybe he saw something in it I didn't. After all, he was the expert.

He laughed, the effort completely changing his face. It made him look younger, more relaxed. "You're joking, right? This shit makes me want to send Alan home for the day in hopes that he returns tomorrow with something more inspired." Alan was one of two senior graphic designers for the agency, and clearly he'd misunderstood Aidan's vision.

"Well, maybe…" What could I say? He was right—it was crap.

"There's a team coming from Blast this afternoon. I want you to take your ideas to creative and ask them to come up with three mock-ups. Tell Alan to pack up his things if he hands over another ad like this one."

I stared at Aidan. "I'm not telling him that. I barely know him. Shouldn't you be the one to take the ideas over?"

His mouth twitched, and the warmth in me reignited. Why did he have to be so sexy? "You do realize you work for me, don't you?"

"Technically, I work for Gayle."

"Who works for me."

He cocked his head slightly, daring me to argue. I had no idea why I was arguing with him. He *was* my boss. For all the convolutedness of our situation, that detail was perfectly clear. But ordering the senior designers in creative to do something for me, an entry-level nobody, ranked high on my I'd-rather-scrub-toilets list.

"Don't worry, they won't bite."

Snatching my phone off his desk, I started for the door. "Fine, but I'm not telling them the firing bit. You can do that yourself." I could almost hear his smile from across the room as I slipped through the door.

· · ·

I stood in line at Starbucks an hour later, desperate for a pick-me-up after my attempts to explain my ideas to Alan and Trent, the designers on the campaign, who did little more than stare at me while I spoke. I still wasn't sure they understood a word I said. Regardless, the Blast Water people would be at our office at one for a lunch meeting, and I wanted to be on my game, show that I was an active part of the team.

My thoughts drifted back to Aidan and his words from his office. I tried not to dissect every moment, but something about him put me on edge. I wanted him to like me, in more ways than I should.

"What do you suggest?" a voice asked from behind me, yanking me from my thoughts. I turned around to see a man dressed in the sort of suit that could max out a credit card. He had deep brown hair and olive skin and a flashy smile that said he knew exactly how he looked and planned to use his looks to their full potential.

"It's Starbucks," I said, teasing. "Something tells me you know how this works." The barista asked for my drink order and I called out my regular grande vanilla latte and motioned for the guy to place his order. I waited for him to say something like venti, double shot, blah, blah, blah, but instead he flashed me a grin again and said to the barista, "I'll have a coffee. Black. Whatever size you think is fine, or better yet, let her decide." His gaze swept from the barista to me, where it held.

I raised my eyebrows, surprised. "Wow, you really are a Starbucks virgin. How does that happen, exactly?"

The man shrugged. "I don't have time for complicated. I always walk in, order a black coffee, and walk out."

"Give him a grande. It's just enough." Then I grabbed my coffee and turned toward the elevators with trepidation. Sure enough, the slowest elevator known to the world opened up, and I didn't have time to wait on my favorite. Damn, slow turtle of an excuse for an elevator. I was just considering taking the stairs when I heard someone walk up behind me.

"I'm a visitor here. Think you could give me directions?"

I pointed to the directory beside the elevator without looking at him. I didn't need this distraction. Not today. "Sorry, I'm new, but that should help." I stepped inside the turtle elevator and turned to see Coffee Dude shaking his head, a crooked grin on his face as the doors closed.

It took ten rounds of "Row, Row, Row Your Boat" to get me to the fifth floor, and by the time I made it to my desk, my hands were shaking, my breathing uneven. *Inhale...exhale... Inhale...exhale.* After a solid minute of this, my breathing relaxed, and I clicked my email, eager for a distraction, but before I could dive in, Gayle appeared at my desk. "Have a minute? The Blast guys are here early."

Crap.

"Um, yeah, sure." We started toward the conference room. "But I don't think creative has had time to fix the mock-ups," I whispered.

"Don't worry. Aidan's going to lead the meeting. His middle name should be bullshit. He'll wow them. Then he'll tell us he's disappointed in our efforts and order an all-nighter until we solidify our idea."

"Great."

She opened the glass door to the conference room and motioned for me to follow her, but my eyes had stopped on the two men already seated at the table. One was older, maybe sixty, and the other was Coffee Dude from downstairs. He smiled knowingly, and I felt my cheeks flush as the guy held out his hand for me to shake. "Trevor Blast."

"Cameron Lawson. So you must be…?"

His father held out his hand for me to shake. He had an air about him that I instantly liked. He reminded me of my stepdad, Eric. He was real, not at all the typical executive. "William."

I glanced between the two men. "Very nice to meet you both. We're so excited to handle your campaign."

They both smiled, and I knew instantly where Trevor inherited his telltale grin. Gayle shook their hands as well and we sat in front of them, me fighting to keep my cheeks from burning and Trevor clearly fighting to keep from laughing. How the hell did I get myself into these situations?

Aidan and Brody came through the door a moment later, saving me from an awkward apology.

"Gentlemen," Aidan said, holding out his hand. He didn't sit. Instead, he let his eyes land on each of us, an act intended simply to show us respect. I loved that about him. He really was amazing at his job.

I glanced up to find Trevor watching me. He flashed me

a smile and mouthed something I couldn't make out, and suddenly, Aidan stopped talking and peered down at me. "Cameron, is there something you want to add?"

"What? Me? No. Not at all." I folded my hands in my lap, praying Trevor would behave, or else I could be off this campaign before it officially began.

Aidan didn't look at me again for the remainder of the meeting, and for once, I was grateful. He launched into three ideas, and then when he started the fourth, my gaze darted up to his to find him watching me, waiting for my reaction. It was one of mine. Creative had used one of mine.

He smiled knowingly and then turned to the screen behind him. It was a flashy commercial with boys playing football as kids and then quickly transforming into men as the video continued. Then the slogan, "Blast Water, turning kids into athletes since 1995." William nodded along during the idea, and at the end, he and Trevor picked two they wanted us to explore. One was clearly an idea Aidan had pulled on a whim, and the other was mine. It was all I could do to keep from screaming in excitement.

William and Trevor stood at the end of the meeting and passed around business cards with the other higher-ups in the room. Just as they were about to leave, Trevor turned back. "Very nice to meet you, Cameron."

I smiled. "Likewise."

As soon as they left, I started around the table, picking up leftover water bottles. Alexa could do it, but I was here, so why not help? My skin began to prickle, and I peered up to find Aidan still in the room, watching me, his hands tucked in his pockets.

"Oh, hey, I thought everyone had left."

He didn't move, and I realized then that he wanted to say something. "Did you know him?"

"Who?"

"Trevor Blast."

"I met him downstairs. Why?" The whole exchange felt off, like he was a jealous boyfriend instead of my boss.

His mouth opened, then closed, then he motioned to the table, like he wasn't sure what else to do. "You don't have to clean up."

"I know. But just because I don't have to doesn't mean I shouldn't help, you know?"

He shook his head. "No one thinks like that."

I stood across from him now, staring over the table, the distance both impossibly long and impossibly short. Were others out in the office, watching us right now? "I do."

He started to speak again, and I paused, waiting to hear what he wanted to say, but he only watched me, then as though he realized what he was doing, he took a step back and ran a hand through his hair, blinking like he'd been in a trance. "They liked your idea. Good work."

"Thanks. It sounds like they liked yours, too."

Aidan shrugged off the compliment. "Ah, it was a throw-in. Yours is the keeper. It's good. Great, actually." He held my gaze, the energy between us building by the second.

I smiled, unable to hide my joy at his praise. Aidan knew advertising. He wouldn't say my idea was good unless it was truly special. The thought made my heart warm, despite my best efforts to stay levelheaded, to remember that he was my boss. He could compliment my work and it meant nothing extra. But this didn't feel like nothing.

Our eyes met once more, the moment so intense it was

almost painful, and then he ran a hand through his hair again and started for the door just as I turned around to trash the bottles I'd picked up. I waited until the door closed before turning back around, my heart a noticeable presence in my chest.

Somehow, UT Guy and Aidan were blending together in my mind. I needed to put a stop to these thoughts before my heart opened up to him. Even if he weren't my boss, this wouldn't work. He didn't date, and I didn't do the casual thing. We would never work.

Chapter Nine

I spent the rest of the afternoon going back and forth between creative and my desk, taking the longest way possible to avoid Aidan's office, afraid to feel that connection between us again. Finally, I closed down my laptop and tucked it into my laptop bag, then grabbed my gym bag and tossed it over my shoulder, eager to head to kickboxing to work off some of this pent-up energy.

The office was quiet, the sounds that filled the air during the busy day now replaced with nothing more than the gentle hum of the air-conditioning. Clearly, early morning and late evening hours would prove to be the best times to work without distractions. I had just turned the corner toward the kill-me-now elevators, right past Aidan's office, when I noticed him standing in front of the Pawel Kuczynski painting, his arms crossed. Beyond the rise and fall of his shoulders, he wasn't moving at all. I watched him, curious what he was thinking, when, as if he could feel my stare, he turned, and our eyes locked, and I swear, even the AC went silent.

Aidan started for his door, and I contemplated turning and going. Nothing about this felt right, yet everything in me told me to stay. "Kickboxing?" he asked.

I lifted the bag. "Yeah, heading there now."

He glanced out his windows, to the darkness that had already set in. "Is your gym close by?"

I shook my head. "No, but it's okay. It's not a terrible walk."

He considered me, then the window again, hesitating. "I don't like the thought of you walking by yourself at night."

The sentiment was sweet, but this was the city. Everyone walked everywhere, and at all hours. It wasn't a big deal. "I'm okay."

He bit his lip, and I wondered what he was struggling with, when he said, "We have a small gym here. A punching bag and gloves. You could practice. Or I could spar with you." His voice dropped as he said the last few words, like he wasn't sure he wanted to say them aloud.

I glanced down the hall to where I knew the gym to be located. This had to be the worst idea on the planet. There was no one else here other than the cleaning crew. No one to see the look Aidan was giving me, equal parts temptation and desire. He took a step toward me, then another, then reached for my laptop bag, easing it off my shoulder. "You can leave your things in my office if you'd like while you go change. I'll meet you in the gym."

"Aidan..." I began, but somehow the words I should say wouldn't come. I eyed the hallway again. Was it my imagination or had it suddenly turned dark and red? The devil stretching out his long fingers and waving me home. Sighing,

I said, "I'll see you in there."

I shut myself into the ladies' room and began to change into my workout clothes—a fitted pink aerobic tank and black yoga pants. The outfit was more than appropriate for the gym, but somehow here, with Aidan, it felt like I had nothing on at all. Every curve I had, both ones I loved and those I hated, were on display for all to see. *It's just a workout*, I told myself as I swept my long blond hair into a high ponytail and glanced at my reflection in the mirror.

My skin was too fair, the few freckles on my cheeks too pronounced, but I had always been the sort of girl who was comfortable in my own skin, grateful for what God had given me. Maybe that was my upbringing coming out, but living in New York could make a perfectly healthy girl feel heavy and a casually dressed girl feel downright tacky. It was exhausting at times, so I'd decided back at NYU that I wouldn't fall prey to those things. I might be fair, but my skin was clear and vibrant. I might be curvier than girls like Alexa, but my large breasts made up for the swell in my backside and hips, giving me an hourglass shape.

Yet somehow all that coaching I'd given myself over the years flew out the window when Aidan looked at me. He made me feel self-conscious and beautiful all at the same time. And knowing he'd seen me naked did little to help.

I pushed open the door at the end of the hall and flicked on the light, exposing the company gym. It was a large room with wall-to-wall mirrors. The treadmills and ellipticals sat to the far left in front of a wall-mounted flat-screen. To the right were free weights and benches for lifting. And then to the right of the door were miscellaneous items, including the punching bag and gloves, yoga mats, jump ropes, and exercise balls.

I walked over to the mats and began to stretch, when the door to the gym opened and Aidan walked in, dressed in loose gray gym shorts that hung low on his narrow hips and a white T-shirt that showed off every taut curve and dip of his chest and arms. A flash of that chest pressed against me, his lips moving with mine, hit in my mind, and I sucked in a shallow breath, then two, trying to calm myself down. It should be illegal for a boss to be this hot. Weren't there regulations for this kind of thing? No one too ripped, no one too young—no one with hair you wanted to run your fingers through while his mouth—

Stop.

Aidan lowered his head as he started for me. Even his walk was sexy. Slow, methodical. Every step so damn controlled. God, I was going to die before this workout even began.

"Did you find everything you needed?" He avoided looking directly at me, and I realized maybe he was as affected by me as I was him.

"I did. This place is amazing." I took a step toward him, testing my theory, and his gaze lifted to my face before sweeping slowly down my body, his expression full of agony.

He cleared his throat and stepped back, his eyes darting away. "So, where should we begin?"

"Warm up?" I walked over to a wide-open space in the middle of the room and continued my stretches. I'd learned long ago that if I didn't take the time to wake my body up I'd pay for it the next day. Aidan watched me sit down on the ground and open my legs wide. "Do you work out in here often?" I asked.

His eyes locked on my legs. "Hmm?"

I fought the urge to grin. "Do you work out here often?"

"Most nights. I mix it up. Free weights or cardio."

I stood up and stretched my arms out, then bent forward to touch my toes. He wasn't stretching. He was watching. And the look in his eyes messed with my body and mind in the best and worst possible ways. In that moment, I'd have given anything for him to be *anyone* other than my boss.

"Are you ready?" he asked.

With a quick nod from me, he walked over to grab two pairs of gloves, then met me in the center of the room and passed a set over to me. He was so close. Too close. My skin hummed and tingled, heat spreading through me. Attraction was one thing, but this was torture.

I slipped the gloves on and backed up, eager for a little distance so I could get my heart to calm down.

"Everything okay?" he asked from across from me, a crooked grin on his face. "Don't worry, I'll go easy on you."

And just like that, my competitive side took over, agitation working through me as I got into position. "Yep. Fine. Good. Let's start." I was totally going to knock that smirk off his face. Forget sparring.

I lunged forward and began moving, but with each punch, he was already there, blocking me. My eyes widened as I stepped back again. "You fight?"

"Not anymore."

"I sense a story there."

He shrugged, and I realized then that he didn't like compliments. They made him uncomfortable. "Not really. I was a black belt in karate when I was younger. Used to compete."

"So, karate is your thing?"

"My thing?"

Kick. Punch. Damn, could he at least let me land something? I pushed harder, growing breathless. "You know," I said, trying to catch my breath. "Your hobby. Your interest."

"Not now. I went through an extreme sports phase right after college—rock climbing, mountain biking, that sort of thing, but I don't really have the time for it anymore. My *interests* have changed." His eyes gleamed with mischievousness.

I laughed. "Yet you refuse to date. What's that about?" I knew I shouldn't question him on his love life, but conversation with Aidan came too easily when we were alone.

"Ah, the question of questions."

"You don't have to answer."

He walked over to a refrigerator in the corner, pulled out two waters, and passed one over to me. Taking a long drink of his, he set the bottle down on the mat, clearly stalling. "Let's just say I don't want to end up like my father. So I take away the possibility. No dating. No risk of marrying and turning out like him."

My breathing slowed as I watched him, searching for something in his face that said his reason was thinner—why date, why get serious, when there were so many women? Something like that. But he only appeared sad. Like the conversation had stirred up memories he didn't want to remember.

"I'm sorry. I shouldn't have asked."

"No, I shouldn't have answered, but with you..." His eyes locked on mine and the charge in the air sparked. "I reveal too much."

"Yeah, I know what you mean."

"What about you? Where do you stand on the relationship thing? Do you date? Have coffee with men who offer?"

He smirked.

I turned away, needing a break from his stare. A break from the intensity building between us. Unscrewing my water bottle, I took a long pull, then two, playing the stalling game myself now.

"I *only* date." I spun to look at him. "I don't do casual. Our thing, it—That was a first for me." Silence replaced the easiness from before, and I wondered if I shouldn't have admitted my feelings. A guy saying he refused to date didn't have the same social implication as a woman saying she only dates.

"Why?"

I met his stare, refusing to be embarrassed. He could want what he wanted, and I could want what I wanted. There was no right. "Because I've seen what it's like to live a life full of love. My parents loved each other, respected each other. And then my dad died and my mom met Eric, and somehow, I was lucky enough to see love in my house for a second time. That kind of love impacts you. You don't want less than the real thing when you've seen it firsthand."

"I guess that's the problem. I've never seen it."

My gaze locked on his, my heartbeat erratic for reasons that had nothing to do with exercise. "I'm sorry for how I acted the day after we were together," I said, my voice low. "For kicking you out and saying you were a twenty-eight-year-old without a job. That wasn't fair."

The corners of his mouth twitched. "You didn't say I was a twenty-eight-year-old without a job."

"Oh. I must have just thought it."

The grin spread and he took a step toward me, humor switching to longing at the mention of our time together. "I had a great time with you. If I did the dating thing, I would have wanted to date you." His eyes darkened, and I held my breath, knowing I should stop this. That he should stop this. One of us should stop this. But I couldn't pull away. His head dipped down, so close I could almost taste the mint on his breath, but then his back went rigid and he backed up, his irises so dark they appeared black. "I...we should probably get going. The cleaning crew will be here soon."

I tried to steady my breathing, calm down my heart, but there was no nursery rhyme to get me through this. A shiver worked its way down my spine as I peered over at him, only to find him biting his lip like it took every bit of strength in his body not to close the distance between us.

Just then the gym door opened, and a cleaning cart came into sight, followed by a small old man. "Sorry. I thought the office was empty."

Aidan's gaze swept from me, and he waved him in. "No, come in. We were just leaving."

I swallowed hard. "Right...just leaving."

Chapter Ten

"So, where do you want to eat lunch?" Alexa stood beside my cube, her bag already slung over her shoulder. I'd already turned her down three days in a row, so I couldn't say no. The problem was I had next to no money in my account. I could afford to spend ten dollars on lunch, which left me with barely enough cash to grab the toilet paper Lauren had asked me to pick up on my way back to our apartment. Everything else was for bills.

I had been on the job for nearly a week, but due to the pay schedule, I wouldn't receive my first check for another week. Which meant I needed to bring my lunches from home, else I'd starve.

Aidan and I had fallen into a professional pattern after the events in the gym. He'd say hi, I'd say hi. Nothing less and nothing more. He was the last person to leave the office every day, and I made it a point to leave with everyone else, so as not to tempt myself into knocking on his door, on looking into those brown eyes and telling him I'd rethought my commitment-girl stance and was willing to do the no-dating thing, break all the rules, whatever, just to feel his lips on mine again.

It was bad enough that I had to work with him every day, but my dreams were becoming a problem all on their own. I had fantasies that could fill the most erotic novel on the planet, and then I would have to see him the next day and pretend that I hadn't just dreamed about him being in my bed.

"So…?" Alexa asked, pulling me back to the moment.

"Right. Yeah, sure, but can we go affordable? I'm kind of tight until payday."

She smiled that sympathetic smile that Grace always flashed to Lauren and me. Alexa's parents owned some major computer software company that I'd never heard of, but apparently it was doing very well.

"I can cover you," she said, causing me to cringe. I hated the idea of anyone helping me out. There was just something about doing it on my own, about suffering, and then finding myself on top at the end of my struggle. "Besides," she said, lowering her voice and glancing around, "I have gossip, and I need someone to share it with."

"About who?" I whispered.

She glanced around again. "Aidan."

Suddenly my insides turned to ice. I grabbed my bag and nodded to Alexa for us to go. A cold front had blown in, making the October air feel like early winter. I shivered beneath my peacoat, wishing I'd opted for pants instead of skirt and boots.

Alexa waited until we were seated at a small sandwich

shop around the corner before blurting out, "Guess who I saw out last night?"

The smells of freshly baked bread filled my nose, making my stomach all the more uncomfortable with this topic. I didn't want to hear what she was going to say next, but it was like a car accident. I couldn't look away. "I'm guessing Aidan?"

A devilish grin spread across her face. Oh God, she was going to tell me that she slept with him, that she'd seen his body in all its glory. I braced myself as she leaned in. "He showed up at that new club, Blaze, last night, and I swear, every woman was trying to talk to him. I'd never seen anything like it. But here's the juicy part." She eyed the shop to make sure none of our coworkers were there, listening to us gossip. "He left with Misha Kyle, the freaking Victoria's Secret model. She went up to him as soon as he walked in, and then they left together. I wouldn't be surprised if photos showed up in the gossip magazines this week."

I forced myself to draw a breath, or else my entire body would turn green with envy. Misha Kyle. I knew next to nothing about modeling, but everyone knew Misha Kyle. She was that girl every girl in America wanted to look like. Long tousled hair, perfect golden skin, legs that went on for days and days. And she was with Aidan. Ugh.

Alexa had said he had a reputation, but I'd never seen it firsthand, so I'd pretended that the rumors were just that— rumors. But Aidan said he didn't date, which meant he only hooked up. Clearly, his latest conquest was Misha Kyle.

She continued to tell me every single detail about Aidan and Misha, and by the time we returned to the office, I was wishing for a touch of amnesia so I could forget everything she'd said. I started back for my desk, desperate to finish this day so I could go out with Grace and Lauren that night and hopefully find a decent guy to distract me, when I heard my name called from behind. I knew that voice. Could I keep walking like I'd never heard him?

"Cameron?"

Dammit.

Turning slowly, I cleared my face of all emotion. Aidan stood in his doorway, wearing a light blue dress shirt and black slacks and looking like he'd just walked off a photo shoot. Probably one where he was naked with Misha. Ugh, ugh, ugh. I had no right to be this upset. He and I weren't a thing. We weren't even friends. But we'd hooked up, and I couldn't undo that in my mind. To me, he would always be UT Guy first, Aidan second.

"Yes?"

Several employees passed before he said another word. He looked around the office and then back to me, like he wasn't sure how to talk to me after the gym. Having sex was one thing, but we'd both exposed pieces of our pasts now. He knew my dad had died, and I knew his wasn't a good man. "Cameron…"

He studied me a moment longer, and I realized I both hated and loved his stare. He stared at you as though you were complex and important. As though his mission in life was to figure you out. It was overwhelming and intoxicating all at the same time. "Creative sent a few quick mock-ups for Blast. Would you like to look them over?"

"Sure." I glanced around for a hard-copy proof, but didn't see one. "Um, sorry, am I missing something?"

Aidan shook his head like he'd been in a daze. "They're

on my computer. I didn't want to wait for hard copies. Do you have a minute?"

"Um, yeah. Yeah, of course." I followed him into his glass office, conscious of how visible we were to the rest of the staff. My thoughts went to the last time we were alone together, the charge between us so intense there was no pulling away. God, I wanted to kiss him. I wanted to do more than just kiss him. Forget the rules and complications, I wanted to wrap my arms around him and see if his body remembered me the way mine so clearly remembered him. I tried to shake the thought from my mind, but it was too late. My body buzzed with desire.

"So, the mock-ups?" I asked, desperate to get in and out of his office as fast as possible.

"Right." He moved his mouse to wake his computer, and instantly the most beautiful ad I had ever seen filled the screen. It was masculine. It was edgy. And it was mine. Something about seeing your idea put into reality was so absolutely breathtaking. Unlike anything I had ever experienced. I covered my mouth with my hand, fighting to keep from squealing with excitement.

On the left was a boy with a Band-Aid under each of his eyes. He was tiny and wearing a football uniform that looked two sizes too big. He had a frown on his face. And then to the right was Charlie Spike. Heisman contender. One of the best quarterbacks in the country. In place of the Band-Aids were two black stripes. He looked fierce and tough, everything a young boy wanted to be when he grew up. It was a perfect transformation. Colored sweat slipped down his face, and at the bottom were the words "Blast Water, turning kids into athletes."

"It's amazing."

"It's a great feeling, huh?"

I studied the ad, and the longer I stared at it, the more I realized something was missing. It looked too manufactured, too fake. It didn't resonate like it should.

Aidan cocked an eyebrow at me. "What?" he asked.

"Nothing. It's just, something isn't right. It's good. Yet, there's something…"

He focused back on the screen, his eyebrows threading together. "You're right. It's close, but we need it to be perfect." He started to say something else, but stopped.

Now it was my turn to ask, "What?"

"Nothing. You—nothing."

I closed my eyes for a second to give me the courage to say what I needed to say next. The tension between us had been excruciating all week. When we were alone in the gym, everything was fine. But being around the office, with the awkward hellos and avoiding each other's eye contact in meetings—enough was enough. We were working in the same office, on the same project. We needed to put that night behind us.

I glanced quickly at the door and then leaned in closer and lowered my voice. "Look, so we had sex. It doesn't have to be a thing. It's nothing. No big deal."

Aidan raised his eyebrows as a slow grin spread across his face. "Actually, I was just going to tell you that you have a little mustard on your cheek. Right there." He pointed at my left cheek, and my entire body burned red and splotchy. There was no containing this embarrassment.

I took a step back, my eyes on anything but him. "Oh, right. Thanks." I swiped at the spot and glanced down at my hand, but nothing came away. I started to go for it again, when he stood and slowly walked toward me. My heartbeat sped up with each step, and then he reached out and ran his thumb across my cheek, sending a surge of tingles from my cheek to my toes. I wanted to look out into our office, check to see if others could see us, but I couldn't bring myself to look away from him. And then he lifted his thumb to his mouth and licked away the mustard, and holy. Hell. My already-heated body burst into flames.

He held my gaze as his arm dropped back to his side. "And it is a big deal. To me. It's all I can think about."

Chapter Eleven

"Aidan, I need your signature on—" Dorothy, Aidan's assistant, stopped inside the door. "I'm sorry, I didn't realize you were in a meeting."

Aidan turned slowly to face Dorothy, his expression as relaxed as ever. "We were just finishing up."

"Okay, thanks, Aidan. I'll get right on this." I sped out of his office and back to my cube, drawing a long breath as I sat down in my chair. *He can't stop thinking about it? As in, he's worried, or he can't stop thinking about me?* It didn't matter. It meant nothing, because we were nothing and never would be any more than nothing. Rules were rules. And he didn't date. Even if the company rule weren't there, I couldn't get involved with him. I'd known my whole life the kind of guy I wanted. A family man, who adored his parents and wanted kids of his own someday. Aidan wasn't my guy.

With the phrase firmly set in my mind, I threw myself into my work. Researching, checking emails, reviewing a few mock-ups creative had sent me for other projects. My phone vibrated against my desk, and I peered over to see a string of texts from Grace and Lauren. I read the trail, my face breaking out into a giant smile with each text.

Grace: *We're going out tonight. Like, hook up, embarrassed-the-next-day, going out.*

Lauren: *I have $0.10 in my bank account. Scratch that. Shit. I'm negative again. Fuck, why does this keep happening to me?*

Grace: *Because, silly girl, you refuse to actually keep a budget. If you'd listen to me, you'd have plenty of money.*

Lauren: *Says the girl WITH plenty of money. Where are you, Cameron? I need to know I'm not alone in the poorhouse.*

I quickly texted back that I, too, had next to nothing in my account and asked if we could go out on Friday instead. It was twenty-four hours away and Lauren's payday. Surely Grace wouldn't argue.

Grace: *Fine, but if you go out tonight without me I'm going to be super pissed.*

Lauren and I both responded at the same time with a *Never*, then I eyed the time and quickly began throwing my things into my bag. It was almost seven now. Where had the day gone? The last thing I wanted was to be stuck here with

Aidan—alone. I wasn't sure I could keep myself from asking him what he'd meant.

I kept my head down as I slipped into the elevator, and began my usual mantra even before the doors had closed. *The itsy bitsy spider went up the waterspout. Down came the rain…*

The doors began to close, and I sang the words louder in my mind, my gaze so focused on the tiled floor I didn't notice that the doors never closed. I glanced up as Aidan slipped inside, and then he saw me, and suddenly the tiny space felt almost unbearable. Heat radiated up my back as he turned to face the doors, directly beside me, his shoulder half an inch from touching mine.

"Cameron," he said, and wow, did I suddenly love the sound of my own name. The way he drew the word out, like he needed to keep it on his lips a little longer. I wanted him to say it again.

For a moment, I forgot my singing, but then the doors closed, and I couldn't think about Aidan, not now. I started the song again in my mind and focused on the floor.

"Are you all right?"

I sucked in a rattled breath. "Of course, why wouldn't I be?" *Out came the sun and dried up all the rain.*

"Cameron, look at me."

I peered over, just as the elevator jerked and came to a halt. My eyes flew over to the numbers, to the doors. Why weren't they opening? Why the hell weren't they opening? My gaze went to the ceiling, then the numbers again, the doors. Oh shit, oh God. No, no, no.

Aidan stepped calmly toward the numbers and hit the one again, but nothing happened. We were stuck. My eyes began to burn, and I bit down on my lip hard to keep from screaming.

"Cameron?" He reached down for the emergency button. "It's all right. You know that, don't you?"

I couldn't look at him. All I could do was nod, but nothing about this was right. Sweat broke out across my forehead and back, my legs shook. In romance novels, authors wrote about this very scene like it was the hottest thing imaginable. Get trapped in an elevator with the man of your dreams, the lights go out, and then sexy times begin. But nothing about this was sexy, and if the lights decided to crap out on me, too, then they may as well call the morgue along with the fire department.

Aidan pulled out his cell and called someone, though service was shitty in elevators, so he wasn't likely to get a call through. He reached for the emergency phone, and I could feel his eyes on me, watching my meltdown. By this point, my entire body was shaking, my mind closing down. All I could think about was how small the space was, how little air. I tried to tell myself there was plenty of oxygen, no one died of lack of oxygen in an elevator, but it was no use. Panic coursed through me, polluting every muscle until I wondered how I remained standing.

I briefly heard Aidan rattle off that the elevator was stuck, in what he guessed to be between floors two and three. He thanked whoever was on the phone, and then I felt him by my side.

"Cameron, look at me."

Swallowing hard, then again because the first time didn't seem to work, I forced myself to glance up. Aidan's face softened, and he reached up, his thumb trailing just under each of my eyes. I hadn't realized the tears had fallen, but I was too afraid to be embarrassed. Too afraid to be anything at all.

"Claustrophobic?"

I gave a sharp nod.

"Do you want me to give you some space? Would that help?"

I thought of the question and drew another breath, but I couldn't seem to get my lungs to work properly. Dear God. I closed my eyes. "Can you just talk to me? Tell me a story. Tell me anything. Just...please. Talk." My legs felt weak, so I slumped down onto the floor and rested my forehead against my knees. Aidan waited a moment, perhaps unsure of where he should sit, what he should do, but then I felt him beside me again. He took my hand in his and traced lines on my palm, each stroke soothing the tension.

"When I was little," he began, "my father used to say that nothing in the world mattered more than how people said your name. Whether they said it with fear or respect or hate or love, the way they said it spoke to who you were as a person. He said if you ever wanted to amount to anything, your goal should be to hear fear or respect, nothing else."

I bit my lip to keep from spouting out exactly what I thought of such an asinine comment, and instead thought of how different his dad was from mine, how my father would have said nothing mattered but how God saw you. That if you were good in God's eyes, then that ought to be enough for anyone else. "Do you agree?" I asked, praying Aidan didn't share his father's extreme views.

"No. But then I disagree with most of what my father says. I think it matters less how people see you and more how you see them. You can learn a lot about a person if you pay attention. You can learn what makes them tick, what makes them more efficient at work, happier in life. You can learn things you would never know otherwise. Things the person would never tell you."

My eyes lifted, and I knew he was reading me the way he explained. I could only imagine what he saw—crazy lady on aisle three! Can't even get on an elevator! Send a cleanup crew!

At least he wasn't laughing. Not out loud, anyway.

I cringed at the thought and focused on the wall across from us, listening as the second hand on my watch *tick, tick, tick*ed loudly, reminding me how long we'd been trapped. I knew it was only a few minutes, ten maybe, but it felt like hours. I swallowed again. "Are you close to your dad?"

He stiffened and looked away. "No, not at all. He left my mother and me when I was eight and never looked back. He's in advertising, too." At my pointed stare, he added, "He's the president and founder of Graham Group."

Wow, I had no idea. Graham Group was Sanderson-Lowe's biggest competitor. Easily the second-largest advertising agency in the world.

"So, your father is…?"

"Stuart Graham. He's the reason I went into advertising. Not because the field interested me at first, but because I wanted to be better than him in every way. A better businessman. A better man. Especially after my mom died."

"I'm sorry about your mom."

He looked away. "It was years ago now."

We fell into silence, and it was then it hit me—this was the no-dating thing. He didn't want to be the kind of man who left his wife, like his father had left his mother. Surely he knew not all men left. There were great men who stayed. Day in and day out, through the tough stuff, they stayed. A thousand questions rushed to my mind, on the tip of my tongue. Questions I wasn't allowed to ask, questions I shouldn't even think. The silence lingered between us.

"How are you feeling?" he asked after a while.

"Better than expected," I admitted. "I like it when you talk. It helps." My cheeks burned at the truth in my words. What would I do if he weren't there with me, helping me through this? I couldn't imagine. I liked to think of myself as a strong, independent person, but this phobia went beyond all reason and explanation. I'd tried everything to coax myself out of it, which was why I still rode elevators—though that little gem of triumph flew out the window the moment this horror began. The likelihood of me ever getting on another one was slim to never.

"I like it when you talk, too," Aidan said, almost in a whisper. "I could listen to your voice all day and never grow tired of it. It's gentle, but sure. I've never known a woman who could come across as delicate and strong all in the same breath."

My heart warmed at his words, at how easily he admitted these things. "What did you mean by what you said in your office?" I asked. Our closeness (and our looming death) made it easy to ask. Who knew if another opportunity would arise?

This time he looked at me. "I want you. Every time you speak, I want you more."

My body went numb, lost on how to respond. Of all the scenarios I'd played out, all the things I thought he might

say, none of them came close to this. But then the elevator jerked again, and my pulse sped up. Visions of crashing to my death ripped through my mind, but then it began
to move down, finally stopping on the first floor, where it
opened, a few firefighters and some of the building techni-
cians there to greet us.

"Everyone all right?" one of them asked.

We both nodded and thanked them, then I rushed for
the door, eager to get outside. I closed my eyes as soon as
the chilly night air crossed my face and drew a long, long
breath. Air. I wanted to cry it felt so good, then I heard the
sound of someone chuckling and peered over.

"And so the laughing begins. I knew it'd come eventually."

He smiled. "Sorry. You just look like you've won the
lottery."

"I did. The oxygen lottery."

"Do you want me to get you a cab?"

This time I laughed. "Another small space? No, thank
you. I'm walking."

Aidan considered me, then the street. "Then I'm walking
with you."

"Aidan, that's not—"

"I'm walking with you."

"All right," I said, unable to keep from smiling. "Fine."

We set off down the sidewalk, the air seeming to cool
down with each passing moment. I loved the city in early
fall, how all my favorite holidays were right around the
corner—Halloween, Thanksgiving, Christmas. I absolutely
loved the city at Christmas.

"Why do you look so happy?" Aidan asked after a few
blocks of walking in silence.

"I love the city, especially this time of year. It's weird, really. My parents are very big on Southern pride, but it never really stuck for me. I remember getting excited when I was little when my parents would tell me we were going on vacation. My dad, my real dad, used to take us all over, but it was like once he died, my mom refused to step foot on a plane and hated being in the car for too long. Some of my friends were going to the Grand Canyon or on a cruise or Disney World. Me? Every year we went one of two places—Panama City or Chattanooga."

"So that's why you came here? To get away from the small-town life?"

I bit my lip, considering the question. "I think I went to NYU to prove that I could. I wasn't some small-town girl, afraid of the city. My mom cried when I told her I'd been accepted, and at first, I thought they were happy tears, but then I realized she wasn't happy for me. She was sad. To this day, moving here was the most disappointing thing I've ever done, in my mom's eyes."

We reached the outside of my apartment building, and I turned to look at him, confused at how I'd once again revealed so much of myself to him. "How do you do that?"

"Do what?"

"Get me to tell you things I never tell anyone. Things I refuse to admit even to myself."

He tilted his head, his gaze penetrating, warming me with that simple look. "I could ask you the same question."

We stared at each other, lost in a moment we shouldn't be having, but I couldn't make myself go inside; I couldn't make myself turn away.

Aidan hesitated, then said, "I can walk you to your door

if you'd like? Ride on the elevator so you're not alone."

"I think it's safe to say my love affair with the elevator has come to an end. It's the stairs and me from now on. Two peas in a pod."

He smiled. "Well then, I'll just—"

"But I'd still like you to walk me to my door."

His gaze drifted down the sidewalk, watching as people went by, and I wasn't sure whether he was checking to see if anyone we knew was around or if he was trying to convince himself to leave. Or convince himself to stay. I prayed for the latter, and then immediately felt like crap. This was my first real job, my first opportunity to prove myself, and here I was risking everything over a guy who didn't date. But right now, standing on the sidewalk, the small trees planted outside my building whipping around in the wind, a cloudy night sky above, all I wanted to do was take this chance.

"It's just a walk," I said.

"You know it's more than that."

I brushed a loose strand of hair from my face, and Aidan watched me tuck it behind my ear like he wished it were his fingertips touching me instead of my own. "So, what are you going to do?"

He took a slow step toward me, invading my personal space, swarming my senses. "I'm going to walk you to your door."

His words repeated in my mind as we slipped into my building—*you know it's more than that*—coiling around and around as we ascended the stairs to the second floor, where I'd insisted Lauren and I live because our building didn't have apartments on the first floor. My heart picked up speed as we passed door after door, my nerves telling me this was wrong, I should thank him and end it there, but I knew I wouldn't. I'd let this go as far as he would take it.

Dear God, let him take it all the way.

I slowed to a stop just before my door and turned to him, unsure if I should invite him inside or say our good-byes now, but then his eyes met mine and he took that delicious step of his. "Why can't I stay away from you?" My breathing slowed as he leaned into my ear. "Your smell, the memory of your warm body under me. It's all I can do to remain still when I'm around you." He pulled away a fraction of an inch, his gaze dropping to my lips. "Ask me to stop. Tell me you don't want this."

"I can't."

"I was afraid you'd say that."

And then his lips were on mine, one hand behind my head and the other pressed against the small of my back, securing me to him. My fingers threaded into his hair, and he moaned lightly into my mouth, making my body quake with need. I fumbled for my door handle and pushed it open, refusing to break the connection between us, but then the sound of loud talking, following by a sharp hush, had Aidan pulling away, his eyes going wide as we took in the scene in my living room. Lauren and Grace and two girls from Lauren's office.

Even my apartment wasn't safe.

Aidan reached for my hand, urging me to face him, and gave me a smile that was supposed to comfort me, but it never touched his eyes. "It looks like you have guests. I should go."

A part of me wanted to beg him to stay, to explain just how well the lock on my bedroom door worked, but I could see the resolve in his face. Whatever magic had taken over in the elevator, and on the walk, and out in the hall, was gone now.

"Okay. Thanks for the walk."

He pressed an easy kiss to my cheek and whispered, "Don't look so disappointed. We still have tomorrow."

"What's tomorrow?"

"The beginning." And he disappeared out my door.

Chapter Twelve

Lauren waited until everyone was gone, including Grace, to corner me just outside my room, her face lit with excitement. "Was that who I think it was?"

I hesitated. Somehow admitting it out loud made the whole thing seem so much worse. "That was Aidan."

She grinned. "Your boss."

"No!" I walked into my room, and she followed. "He's my boss's boss."

"Oh, well, now that we cleared that up."

I kicked off my ballet flats and sat down on the edge of my bed. "What am I doing, L? I can't seem to stay away. First the gym, now this. I could get fired. *We* could get fired."

"Maybe that's why you like it. It has that forbidden thing going on."

"Maybe, but I think it's more than that. I listen to him talk about his life and it just doesn't match the guy I see at the office. He's more than his title, and I can't get enough. I want to know everything about him."

"So why don't you just go for it, but keep it a secret?"

My eyes snapped up. "A secret?"

Lauren walked over and sat on my bed, crossing her legs up under her. "You know, like a secret affair. Behind closed doors. All that movie crap. If you like him, hang out with him, but don't tell anyone. Seriously, this is exactly what you need. You want to focus on your career, right? But you're a woman who has needs. You can have both—the career and the comfort of a man, without all the complications of dating. You don't have to explain late nights at the office or why you're focused more on your laptop or phone than him. It's perfect."

"I don't know." The idea was tempting, but no matter how I reworked the situation, it felt off. I didn't want to tiptoe around with some guy. That wasn't me.

"Cameron, you haven't gone out with a guy since Jacob Warner, and that was months ago. And he was Dr. Phillips's son." She shuddered, and I drew a face.

"Hey, he was hot in a sweater-vest kind of way." I relented at Lauren's pointed stare. "Fine, he was horrible. They were all horrible." I thought of all the dates I'd been on after Blaine. The frat guys. The athletes. The professors' sons. Nothing clicked.

"Not all of them. Blaine wasn't bad. He just wasn't the one." Lauren drew out a long yawn and pushed herself off my bed. "I'm heading on to bed. But think about it. You don't have to make this a thing. You can just have fun," she said around another yawn.

"Yeah, and what about you? What happened with the new boy, Patrick?"

She grinned. "To be determined."

I smiled back. "Tease."

"You know it."

Then I slipped into bed and thought about the word "beginning" and Aidan's lips and how very much I hoped tonight was the beginning of many more to come.

Chapter Thirteen

I walked through the revolving doors of my office building, my mind still replaying the kiss from last night. How it seemed to warm every part of me, even long after Aidan had gone. I wanted to feel his lips on mine again, test the connection. It had been a long time since a kiss had stayed with me. Would a second kiss have the same effect?

Smiling, I slipped through the stairwell door, prepared to suffer the five flights up to Sanderson-Lowe's floor, and came to a stop.

"I hope that smile's for me," Aidan said as he pushed away from the wall. He wore a black suit, tailored to perfection so it showed off his lean, athletic frame, and a white dress shirt with a red tie. Something about a red tie oozed power and control, and suddenly, my mind was envisioning that tie wrapped around my wrists, Aidan kissing a trail down to my—

"Cameron?"

I took a step forward, reaching out to touch the front of his suit jacket before I remembered where we were and stopped myself. "Sorry, I couldn't help it."

He grinned and edged closer. "No one takes the stairs. We're alone."

"How alone?"

Another step. "Alone enough to do this." He leaned down, his minty breath warm on my lips, before his mouth covered mine. I gripped his jacket, holding him to me, and he chuckled against my mouth.

"You're going to get me fired, you know that, right? I'm not going to be able to keep my hands off you at the office. Prepare for lots of private meetings." He kissed me again. "In private rooms." His tongue swept over my lips before dipping inside my mouth, teasing me. "With lots of private attention."

I moaned. "Dear God, you're killing me."

Aidan pulled away to look at me, his eyebrows drawn. "Seriously, though, are you okay with this?"

"What do you mean?"

"I like you. I want to spend time with you. But I'm still not willing to—"

"Commit." My eyes found the floor. "So there will be others. You'll be with others. Like Misha Kyle."

He jolted back. "What?"

"Misha Kyle. You went out with her."

His eyebrows went up. "I did?"

"Yes, Alexa saw you two together at—" I waved my hands in the air. "It doesn't matter. It's none of my business."

"Misha is a longtime friend. She and I met up a few weeks ago to discuss her modeling in a photo shoot for one of our clients." He lifted my chin and peered into my eyes, searching. "I haven't been with another woman since I met you, but if we do this, it has to be a secret, and it has to be casual. I can't allow it to be anything more. And I won't take another step with you until I know you understand this and are okay with it."

I thought of other guys I might meet in the city. Wouldn't those dates operate on these same rules? Well, not the secret part. But no one went out on a date with the assumption they were dating the person they would marry. It was always casual to begin with, and then if the match was there, it'd turn serious. This could follow that path, too. Plus, Lauren had been right last night. My focus was on my career, not dating. Still...

"Maybe we should set some ground rules?"

"Like?"

"Like nothing on office property."

Aidan motioned around the empty stairwell, and I laughed. "All right. So nothing on our floor. And—" I paused, needing to build my courage. "We don't try to label it." I felt stupid saying it like that. Of course there were no labels. But I needed to say it out loud if I hoped to keep my own emotions in check. My job was important to me. I couldn't allow this to mess up everything I'd worked for, but I also couldn't ignore the chemistry between us. I hadn't felt a spark like this in a long time, maybe ever. If there were no labels, then maybe it wouldn't feel so wrong.

He stared down at me, as though trying to find something in my expression, something that gave me away, but I was good at holding in my emotions. Keeping my face straight. I'd become a master at it after my dad died.

"All right," he finally said. "But I have a few rules of my

own."

My eyebrows shot up in question, and he edged closer to me. "No romance. No talking about feelings." My body stilled. "It complicates things, and this is complicated enough."

I thought again of my talk with Lauren the night before, how easy it would be to step into this with Aidan, and before my doubts could convince me otherwise, I said, "Okay."

"Okay?"

"I said okay, didn't I?"

He smirked. "You did. I'm just not sure you mean it."

Ignoring him, I pushed on. "Any others?"

"No meeting family or friends."

This one was easier to digest. I could only imagine my mother's face if I brought Aidan home. *This is my boss. We're kissing and will likely have sex. Again. But nothing serious. Just sex.*

"All right. No romance. No family or friends. Anything else?"

He shook his head. "No. You?"

"No, though I'm sure I'll think of something."

Aidan laughed. "I'm sure you will."

We made our way up the stairs, careful to keep a bit of distance just in case we stumbled upon someone, but Aidan was right, the stairwell remained empty. I walked through the door first, said hello to Alexa and that I would see her in the break room for coffee soon, then walked straight to my cube, ducking inside like I was a criminal on the run. Thoughts began circling through my head. *Surely there were cameras in that stairwell. Anyone could have seen.* But then my cell vibrated with a text and I picked it up to find a number I didn't recognize.

The contact list serves a purpose after all.

I grinned as I added Aidan's cell to my contacts.

Stalking me, I see.

Aidan: *Oh, you have no idea how badly I want to stalk you right now. You look amazing in blue.*

I peered down at my sweater. It was a basic V-neck, but it had a funky boyfriend vibe that I loved. I started to type back something flirty, when I noticed Gayle beside my cube and jumped.

"Are you all right? I didn't mean to startle you."

Faking a smile, I tucked my cell into my bag, my heart pounding. Had she seen Aidan's name on my phone? Surely not. Still, I needed to be more careful. "Um, yes. Fine. Can I help you with something?" I waited.

"We're meeting in about ten minutes in the conference room to go over the campaign. Blast wants us to present in two weeks."

"Sure." I waited for Gayle to leave, and then reached for my phone, expecting to see a text from Aidan. Instead, I found this:

Mom: *DON'T YOU KNOW HOW TO USE YOUR PHONE? WHY ARE YOU IGNORING ME? WHEN ARE YOU COMING HOME AGAIN? THANKSGIVING? CALL ME!*

I hadn't yet determined if Mom was angry with me all the time, or if she simply preferred to text in all caps. Or maybe she'd somehow set her phone to caps and wasn't sure how to undo it.

I pictured my mom waiting for my call, angry that I hadn't talked to her in two days. I mean, seriously, Lauren spoke to her parents once every few weeks, but my mom acted like I'd committed the sin of all sins if I sent her to voicemail, which I never did because then that all-caps text would turn into an all-caps phone call, and my ears had heard enough shrill screams from my mom to last me a lifetime.

I contemplated sending her a quick text now or waiting until after my meeting, when another text came through.

Eric: *Have mercy on an old man. Call your mother before she drives me to drink. Again.*

I smiled. Eric hadn't drunk a drop of alcohol since he returned from Desert Storm. He used to tell me stories of his father, a World War II veteran, with horrible PTSD. He drank so much that he was convinced Eric and his brothers and sisters (eight of them in all) were Japanese military. So when Eric came home from his own war, he vowed to never drink. To never be his daddy. It was one of a thousand reasons why Eric was the best man I knew and one of my favorite people. I loved him like a father, even if the thought made me feel guilty inside. He was good to my mom, and he loved her...which wasn't always the easiest thing to do.

I stood up and peered over my cube to the conference room, where Gayle and creative were already seated. Dang it. I quickly texted to Mom, *So sorry. Call you after work today?* Then I remembered that I was going out with Lauren and Grace. I'd have to call her before we went out.

When I arrived at the conference room, everyone was

already there, including Aidan. I purposefully chose to sit at the exact opposite end of the table from him, sure that I couldn't trust myself to sit in the only other empty chair—the one directly beside him. Aidan gave me a knowing grin as I sat down, then launched into the meeting. I listened as he went over the final campaign, watched as his full lips moved, and then my thoughts went south. I remembered the feel of them on my cheek, my neck, the sound of him moaning into my mouth. *Dear God…*

"Cameron?"

I blinked. "Yes?"

Everyone at the table was staring at me, clearly waiting for me to answer some question I hadn't heard. Shit. I tried to remember what had just been said, who had been speaking, anything, but all I could think about was making out in the stairwell after the meeting. This was a problem. A serious, serious problem. New rule: no unbelievable kisses before work.

"Are you with us?" Aidan asked, his eyes flashing. All devil and sin.

I glared at him, before glancing back at Gayle. "Sorry, can you repeat that? I was—"

"Distracted?" Aidan added, his expression even. He knew exactly what I was thinking about. Damn him.

Gayle gave me a comforting look. I felt sure if she knew the underlying meaning behind this little exchange she wouldn't be so comforting. "I asked what you thought of the latest mock-up."

I considered the images on the screen behind Aidan. Beyond font changes, it was virtually the same as the one he'd shown me in his office. Something was still off. My mouth opened to say that it was good, to tuck away my true thoughts until I was more established with the company, but that attitude wouldn't help me move up. I had to be sharp, and part of being sharp was knowing when to voice your opinion and when to keep your mouth shut. This was definitely a time to speak up.

"It's very good," I said, nodding to creative, because I'd learned they liked to have their egos stroked. "But I think something's missing. Maybe…" I cocked my head as I studied the mock-up. "Maybe the kid shots need to be actual photos of the players as children. That kid looks nothing like the player. I think to really give this that emotional punch we're looking for they need to at least *appear* to be the same person." I waited for Aidan's reaction. "And we should see them aging. Like a montage from kiddie teams to high school to college."

He released a slow breath. He was thinking about it, letting it churn around in his mind. Finally he focused on creative. "Let's add in photos from actual players. If you can't get them, find stock photos that are closer to the players. I want them so close they'd fool their mothers." The guys from creative took notes on their iPads, and then Aidan nodded to me. "Good work."

"Thanks," I said, a grin spreading across my face that I couldn't contain. Suddenly, I was reminded how much I loved advertising and how much I loved this job. While Aidan's no-romance–no-emotions rule cut deep, I knew he was right. My focus was on my career, and I couldn't allow whatever this was to jeopardize everything I'd worked so hard to obtain.

Aidan ended the meeting, and as we were all walking

out, Alexa stopped me. "Lunch?"

I eyed my phone. Sure enough, it was nearly noon. "Sure." My bank account would hate me for eating out again, and I knew just what Grace would say—why not dip into your dad's money? Just a little won't hurt. What are you going to do with it anyway?

I'd heard that very question a thousand times, and it never became easier to answer. The truth was I didn't feel right buying anything at all with the money. I didn't want it. I wanted him, alive. So I'd resigned myself that I wouldn't spend a dollar of the money until I had something important to spend it on. Something life-changing. Something that would make him proud. I'd yet to find such a thing, so the money sat untouched. Besides, there was something rewarding in doing it all on my own.

Alexa went for the elevator, and I stopped cold. "Yeah, I'm not stepping foot on that thing. I got stuck in it last night."

Her eyes went wide. "Are you serious? Why didn't you tell me?"

I shrugged. *Because Aidan kissed me last night and this morning and I can't seem to think about anything else.* "I don't know. I guess it slipped my mind."

She went toward the stairs. "Oh my God. Was there anyone else in there with you?"

I paused, unsure if I should lie about Aidan or tell her the truth. It wasn't like we'd had sex in the elevator. "Actually, yeah. Aidan."

"Holy shit." Alexa spun to look at me. "You were stuck in an elevator with Aidan? What happened? Please tell me something happened."

Why didn't I just lie?

We were outside now, walking down the chaotic sidewalk, everyone out and about, and she was still waiting for my response.

"We barely talked, and then the elevator was fixed. It wasn't a big deal."

No, it was a *huge* deal. Aidan was caring and sweet and so open about his life. It was a different side of him—a side I wanted to get to know a lot better. The thought made my insides tingle with excitement. UT Guy and Aidan were blending together in my mind, each bit of information I had about him helping to put the pieces together. Aidan was professional at the office, driven and smart. But he was still a twentysomething guy and acted as such in his free time. UT Guy was his after-work persona, the real him when he didn't have to be on. And didn't we all have those two sides?

We sat down for lunch and ordered salads; all the while I longed for fried chicken and mac and cheese. For a moment, I missed home. I missed the constant smells of something cooking from our kitchen, Mom's voice as she sang along to some tune on the radio. Our house wasn't grand, but it was a happy place to grow up.

"So no hot make-out sessions in the elevator, then?"

"With who?" Lauren asked as she and Grace sat down to join us, both on extended lunch breaks—aka their bosses were out of the office. I introduced them and then returned to my salad.

"With Aidan, our boss," Alexa answered with a laugh. As though the possibility were absurd.

I shook my head and smiled. "Sorry to disappoint you. No elevator make-out sessions to report."

We preferred the stairs.

Chapter Fourteen

Lauren and Grace were already at the bar that night, ordering drinks, before I could ask if one of us should stay sober. You know, as lookout. Or maybe just because I wasn't feeling the go-wild vibe Lauren and Grace had sung the entire walk over.

We'd agreed to stop by True Heat, a new club that had opened up and was touted to have the best apple martinis in the city. Apple martinis were to our group what cosmopolitans were to *Sex and the City*, so there we were, eager to see if we agreed. The problem was that while I loved my friends, I didn't want to have random guys talking to me, dancing with me, trying to get me back to their apartments. My mind was on one guy. And that realization was freaking me out.

I'd spent the rest of my afternoon in creative, working through the final campaign additions, and then when I finally returned to my desk, Aidan's light was off in his office.

He'd gone for the day without even a text good-bye. I tried not to read too much into it. We weren't anything, barely enough to even call us a something, yet it felt very much like a *something* to me. No romance, no feelings. *No labels*, I reminded myself. Though I knew I was already labeling us.

I stepped up to the bar and smiled as Lauren handed me the signature apple martini. "It's orgasmic. Try it."

I took a sip, then two, moaning for effect. "Wow. I think I need a cigarette now."

She grinned. "Oh, you will after you see what we've found." She leaned in closer and pointed to her left to a table of guys, Grace already talking away to one of them. The other two were staring at Lauren and me. A few weeks ago, I would have been stoked at the possibility of meeting someone new, but now? My insides felt as though they'd been flipped upside down and weren't quite sure how to work.

"You must be Cameron," the guy nearest to me said. He had thick dark hair and dark eyes and the sort of eyelashes that made girls want to weep from jealousy. He was cute, but beyond that, I felt nothing for him at all—no excitement at the potential. No interest in learning more about him.

"I am," I said. "But I didn't catch your name."

He held out his hand. "Eli. Your friend told me you're in advertising. I'm a graphic designer at GG."

GG—aka Graham Group. Just the name made me uneasy after hearing Aidan talk about his dad.

"Ah, good firm," I said, already wishing I could get out of the conversation.

"Where do you work?"

"Sanderson-Lowe." I peered around to see if the girls wanted to go dance, only to find them already on the dance floor. Crap.

Eli leaned in closer. "We're competitors," he said, his eyes flashing with mischievousness.

Yeah, not happening.

I motioned to the dance floor. "I'm just going to go find my friends."

"I'll come with you."

And now this was turning into one of those scenes in the movies, where the girl was stuck with the weird guy, when she wanted to be with her soul mate, and then soul mate guy walked in and swept her off her feet. Only, my guy wasn't going to walk in and he certainly wasn't going to sweep me off my feet. The thought made me sad for reasons I couldn't fully understand. Didn't I want to focus on my career? Wasn't I the one who said no labels? So why did none of those ideals seem right to me anymore? The truth was deep down I wanted it all—the career and the soul mate. I just wasn't sure that was reality.

My thoughts cut short at the feel of a hand on my stomach. I started to turn just as Eli pulled me flush against his chest, his body moving before I realized that he was trying to dance with me. If pressing your bulge against a girl counted as dancing. I bit my lip to keep from cringing audibly. My gaze darted over to Lauren and Grace, but they were actually into their guys, laughing and flirting and having too good of a time for me to ruin it. I tried to keep pace with the bulge-presser, moving my hips as I took a step away from him, only to have him match my step, securing me to him. Ugh. I spun, dancing around him, which was clearly the wrong thing to do, because now he was looking at me like I was some sex kitten in his latest fantasy. *God, get me out of here.*

I took a step away and reached into my back pocket for my cell, glad that I'd opted for skinny jeans instead of the dress Lauren begged me to wear. My eyes widened as I peered down at my phone. "Sorry, I have to take, uh, *make* a call."

"Now?" He looked like a five-year-old who'd just had his birthday balloon popped.

"Sorry." I pushed through the crowd, toward the bathroom, and clicked my phone, intending to fake a call, but then my eyes zeroed in on the missed text on my screen.

Aidan: *Sorry, had to leave work early to meet with a client. Are you around tonight?*

He'd sent it over an hour ago. I quickly typed back that I was at the club and wished he were with me. There. I could say things without getting romantic, without confessing my feelings. A moment later my phone flashed again.

Then I'm on my way.

I straightened, sure that he was joking. What if someone we knew saw us out? But then I remembered that we were in a city of over eight million people. The likelihood wasn't there.

The line to the bathroom took forever, so when I came out twenty minutes later, I had to scan the club in search of Lauren or Grace. Finally I spotted them and started over, but then my gaze caught on someone at the bar. A giant smile spread across my face, and I tried to rein it in before I reached him. Aidan.

He was dressed in jeans and a button-down, his hair

messy; a fine stubble covered his perfect face. I wanted to run my fingers across his jaw, feel its roughness. But then the bulge-pusher, Eli, cut in front of me, and I blinked to regain focus.

"You disappeared on me," he said.

I faked a smile. He really seemed to be a nice guy. A horrible dancer, but nice all the same. "Sorry. I was just going to meet a friend."

I motioned to the bar, and he turned, scanned the people there, and then his eyes went wide. "Is that Aidan Truitt?"

I sucked in a breath.

"Is he coming over here?"

"He's my boss. He's probably just coming to say hello," I said, hoping my voice sounded more even than it felt.

"You work for Aidan Truitt?"

"Sure. What does it matter?"

He shrugged. "Nothing. I just know his name, his story. How he refused to come work with his dad's company and instead went to the competitor. Seems pretty low if you ask me."

I gritted my teeth together. "You don't know him, so maybe you shouldn't judge."

Aidan arrived before I could say another word. He started for my hand, but I managed to slip out of reach without it looking too obvious. "Aidan, hi, funny running into you here." He gave me a quizzical look, so I quickly added, "This is Eli. He works at Graham Group."

Realization crossed Aidan's face, and then he was all business. He lifted his hand to shake Eli's. "Nice meeting you."

Eli launched into a thousand questions, everything from

Aidan's advertising philosophy, to his political preferences, to his favorite gym. After a while, I felt embarrassed for the guy and desperate to be free from his crazy questioning and dance skills.

"Well, it was nice meeting you, Eli. And I'll see you Monday, Aidan. I was just heading out."

I started to go around them when Eli grabbed my arm. "Are you sure you're ready to go?"

My gaze fixed on him as I pulled free from his grasp. "I'm sure."

"But, we were—"

Aidan stepped between us, forcing Eli to take a step back. "She said she's leaving. Now allow her to leave."

Eli threw up his hands. "Yeah, all right. Of course. Another time, then, Cameron."

I breathed in Aidan's clean scent, and then he said goodbye to me, too, and disappeared through the crowd. My heart sped up as I quickly texted Lauren that I wanted to leave. That was…wow. Aidan stood up for me like I was his—

I shook the thought from my mind before it could fully form when my phone buzzed.

Aidan: *Coffee? There's a small café a block away. Shouldn't be busy at this hour.*

Is that risky?

Aidan: *Yes.*

Aidan: *But you're worth it.*

My heart began to dance as I reread his words. *Why don't we go to my apartment instead? Lauren's out for a while, and I make the best hot chocolate in the world.*

"With whipped cream?"

I spun around to find Aidan behind me, a sexy smirk on his face as he leaned in closer. Warmth pooled low in my belly, spreading through me as I stared into his eyes. Whipped cream and Aidan. This could get interesting. "Is there any other way?"

The smirk turned into a full smile, and I found myself appreciating how it changed his face. How the intense expression he wore at work turned playful and fun. "Ready?"

I nodded. "Can we walk together?"

His gaze dropped to my lips as I spoke, and the warmth in my belly lit on fire, swarming through me, every fiber in me itching to take that tiny step between us, to press my lips to his.

He chuckled lightly and my gaze snapped up. "What?"

"Nothing. Let's go."

We made our way toward my apartment, walking close but not touching. "Thanks for the save back at the club." My fingers ached to reach out to him, to hold hands as we walked. *No feelings*, I reminded myself, but my heart refused to slow down.

We stepped inside my building, and Aidan veered toward the stairs without my having to say a word.

"No problem. He didn't seem like your type anyway."

I smiled. "Oh, yeah? And what's my type?"

"Taller. Blond-ish. Willing to avoid elevators for you."

My smile widened. "That's a very important trait."

He held the door to the second floor open and then

followed me down the hall to my apartment. I unlocked the door and flicked on the lights before tossing my keys in the key basket and glancing around. Lauren and I kept the place pretty clean, but she'd recently taken up crocheting and often had yarn all over the tables. Thankfully, there was none in sight.

"So, hot chocolate, huh?" he asked, as he cocked a hip against the kitchen counter.

I laughed. "I have wine, too, if you prefer."

He moved over to the space beside me and crossed his arms over his chest, making his biceps bulge against the thin fabric of his button-down. "Hot chocolate is good."

Setting the milk steamer on the stove top, I reached for the rest of the ingredients, conscious of his eyes on me as I moved. It was intimidating, but also unbelievably hot to know that he was watching me.

"Nutella?"

"Trust me."

"I trust you more than I should. More than most people I know."

My gaze lifted, and I realized I felt the same way. I shouldn't trust Aidan—I barely knew him—yet our conversations were so effortless that I found myself spilling parts of my life that very few people knew. "We don't really know each other, do we?"

"I know you, Cameron. I see you. You're smart and driven, but your drive isn't like other people's drive. Titles motivate people. Money. But you? You're driven by your independence. Your ability to say you did it all by yourself. Do you have any idea how rare that is for someone your age? Hell, for any age."

"You talk like you've been working your whole life."

"It feels like I've been working my whole life. I used to go to the office with my dad when I was a kid, listen as he ordered people around like they were nothing." He paused, losing focus as he stared across the kitchen. "Then he left my mom and me, and we became nothing. At least to him."

I glanced up as I stirred the ingredients into the already steaming milk. "You weren't nothing."

"No, but we had nothing. No money. Moving from apartment to apartment because she couldn't afford rent and would eventually get kicked out, all while he vacationed at his house in the Hamptons, refusing to pay child support. I know what it's like to have no food, no home, and to have to work every hour to prove myself, only to see flashy Harvard grads walk in and expect the world." He stopped, and I glanced up again from my chocolaty creation.

Mom had taught me how to make the recipe years ago, and it was still my favorite. My heart tugged at the memory of the first time we made it together, her smiling, as beautiful as ever, me standing on a stool so I could see. My heart ached again. It'd been months since I'd been home. Too long. Listening to Aidan talk about his horrible upbringing made me appreciate the life and love my parents had given me all the more.

"What?" I asked after he didn't continue.

"Nothing. I've just never admitted that to anyone before."

I poured our hot chocolate into mugs and turned around to pull the whipped cream from the fridge. It was Reddi-wip, nothing special, but it would serve its purpose. I shook the can and began spiraling it onto the steaming drink when I felt Aidan step up behind me, his head over my shoulder, his strong chest against my back. He placed his hands on my hips, his fingers splaying around to my stomach as he leaned down to press a single kiss to my neck.

I drew a breath. "I like when you do that."

He kissed my neck again. "This?"

"No." I turned around to face him. "I like when you let down your guard around me. When you tell me about your life, and then you draw close, like…" I shook my head, embarrassed to say what I was thinking. I could be wrong.

He lifted my chin. "Like what?"

I swallowed hard as my eyes met his. This close, I could see the flecks of gold in the brown, how they seemed to move every time he blinked. "Like you feel better when you're near me."

He released a breath. "I feel alive when I'm near you." And then his lips were on mine, gentle this time, careful, full of emotions we weren't ready to explore. Emotions we weren't supposed to have. A tingly sensation moved through me, clouding my mind, and I rose onto my toes, not wanting the kiss to end. Not wanting this—whatever we were—to end. The feeling overwhelmed me.

I parted my lips, and Aidan pulled me flush against him, his tongue slipping inside my mouth. He took his time, exploring my tongue, my teeth, my lips, never rushing the kiss. It wasn't urgent or full of want. It was something else, something deeper. His hands moved down my back, and a shiver rippled through me. Lauren could be home any minute, which meant I had a decision to make—either move this to my bedroom and explore Aidan in all the ways I craved, or pull away now and tread cautiously instead. Protect my emotions, my heart.

"Cameron…" he whispered, the words spoken against my lips. "This—it's…"

I pulled away from him so I could better read his expression. "Are you afraid?"

His eyebrows drew together. "Afraid?"

"Of what could happen at the office if we continue this."

Aidan cupped the sides of my face with his hands and stared into my eyes as though he were searching for the answer in me instead of himself. "The only thing in life that's ever scared me is the fear of missing something. A deal. An opportunity." He kissed me softly. "You. I don't want to miss this."

"But, what if—"

He kissed me again before I could continue. "Let me worry about the what-ifs. I won't let anything happen to you. If it falls, it falls on me."

My heart puddled onto the floor, and I realized I was afraid of the same thing—missing this. Despite his rules and mine, I didn't want to miss this. For the first time in forever, I had that tingly feeling in my gut, that nervous ache for the next visit, the urge to smile anytime I heard his name. I finally had all those things, and I didn't want to give them up. Risk or not. This might not be forever, but what was? What really lasted forever? Nothing. No one. The best we could do was live wholeheartedly in the few moments that genuinely made us happy.

Aidan made me happy. Label or no label, feelings or no feelings.

I smiled.

"Is that for me?" he asked, his own mouth curving up into a grin.

"Lately, they're all for you."

His smile softened as our gazes held, and he had just begun the lean-in when I heard a key in the door and then voices. For a moment, I contemplated just introducing Lauren and Grace to Aidan, despite our no friends or family rule. But then they were inside the small hallway, barely out of view, and another voice hit my ears, this one sending me into full freak-out mode. I shoved Aidan back, my eyes wide as I frantically motioned for the pantry door. He shook his head no, and I nodded yes, and I was ready to scream at him to get in there, when Lauren called Alexa's name, and understanding crossed Aidan's face.

I had just enough time to close the pantry door before they walked into the kitchen, feet away from the very spot Aidan and I had been kissing moments before. My heart sped up as my hands trembled from the adrenaline rush.

"Hey," I said, the tightest, fakest smile known to woman-kind on my face. *Dear God, get me out of this and I will go to church every Sunday for the next month.* The girls stared at me like I'd sprung horns. *All right, fine, the next year. Please, God, come on.*

"Um, hey," Lauren said, drawing out the *y.* "We ran into Alexa at the club and decided to just come back here for drinks. You okay?"

Grace turned around to grab wineglasses and a bottle from the fridge.

"I can help," Alexa said, grabbing the glasses so Grace could uncork the wine.

My eyes widened at Lauren, and I nodded toward the pantry door, but she just shook her head like I was insane. "What are you…?"

I pointed at the hot chocolate, still untouched on the

counter. Lauren shrugged, so I pointed again at the two mugs, then the pantry door. *Please understand what I'm freaking telling you!* She shrugged, and I was sure my body was going to explode from tension and frustration, when she glanced at the mugs again and then her eyes went wide and she whispered, "Is there a dude in our pantry?"

I nodded slowly.

Her eyebrows threaded together. "Why?"

Alexa and Grace went on into the living room, and I jerked Lauren toward me. "Aidan is in the pantry. Alexa works at our office, remember? I need you to get her out of here."

She glanced back. "I can't just throw her out."

"Hey," Grace called. "What are you two talking about in there?"

"Nothing!" we both shouted, and I closed my eyes. *Oh my God. This wasn't happening.* Then a genius idea occurred to me. "Take her to your room."

"What? No. That was only the one time in college. I don't—"

I rolled my eyes. "Not to hook up with her. God. Go show her those shoes and bags you brought home from work the other day. She's crazy about fashion. She'll love it."

Lauren looked more mortified than when she thought I wanted her to seduce Alexa. "What if she wants me to give her something?"

I almost laughed at Lauren's blatant selfishness, but then I thought of Aidan on the other side of the door and panic ripped through me again. "Please."

"All right, but if she takes something, you're buying me a replacement."

"Fine, whatever, just please go."

Lauren disappeared out of the kitchen, and I heard her

explain she'd brought home a few things from Bergdorf's that had been sent to her boss in hopes he would agree to carry them the next season. A second passed, then just as I suspected, Alexa asked if she could see them, and they were all heading to Lauren's room. I waited until Lauren's door clicked shut, then yanked open the pantry door and began dragging Aidan to the front door.

"Wait," he said.

I pushed him toward the hallway. "You have to go. She could see you."

He stared at the door, then back at me. "Come with me, then."

"To your apartment?"

"Yes." He took a step toward me. "No roommates. Just you and me."

Voices carried from the other side of the door, pushing my already-jumpy heart to a near heart-attack state. "I can't right now. They'll know something's up."

"Lauren and Grace already know, right?"

"Yes, but I'm not worried about them."

He sighed heavily. "You're staying."

"I have to."

"All right." He reached for my hand and tugged me closer, kissing my lips easily before pulling away. "Then stay with me tomorrow night. We can do whatever you want. Takeout. Movie. Whatever. But stay with me."

A thousand thoughts swarmed through my mind all at once—worries and doubts, excitement and intrigue. Could I keep to the rules if we spent time together alone? But despite my uncertainty, only one word managed to break free.

"Okay."

Chapter Fifteen

Aidan texted me his address the next day after I refused to allow him to take a cab over to pick me up. The day was intense enough without my having to worry about cleaning up or explaining why Lauren was still in her PJs at five. And normally on a dreary day like today, I'd be right there with her, but instead, I was walking into Aidan's apartment building, nervousness and excitement coursing through me in even turns.

I adjusted my overnight bag on my shoulder and peered around for the stairs when my gaze caught on the man leaning against the wall beside the stairwell door. A smile stretched across my face.

Aidan.

He wore loose jeans, an old University of Tennessee T-shirt, and the UT hat from the first time we met. His hair stuck out from below the hat in a disheveled mess, and he clearly hadn't shaven since Friday morning for work, but damn if this look wasn't the sexiest thing I'd ever seen on him.

"Did you adopt my phobia?" I asked as I neared. "Or are you being intentionally sweet?"

He pushed away from the wall and grabbed my bag off my shoulder. "I've adopted a few terrible habits since you threw yourself at me at that bar. It's starting to become a problem."

"Hey," I said, pushing his chest, but then I felt the tightness of his pectoral muscle, and suddenly my thoughts were no longer so light. Aidan's gaze locked on me as he took my hand and ran his fingers easily through mine, causing the fire in my stomach to roar to life. Oh my, this was going to be a very, very dangerous night. I reminded myself to stick to our rules. Everything would be okay so long as I stuck to the rules.

"What are those?" Aidan asked as we started up the steps.

"Brownies."

His eyebrows lifted. "You bake?"

"Only Southern food and baked goods. You can call me Paula Deen if you'd like."

He smirked that sexy grin I loved. "I have a few other names in mind right now, but we'll save those for later."

Later? Oh, my, my, my.

The stairs continued up forever, and guilt worked through my stomach at Aidan suffering on my account. I had just decided to tell him to take the next floor's elevator, I'd see him up there eventually, when he opened the door to level twelve and held it open for me. "After you."

"You just walked up twelve flights of stairs for me."

"I find myself willing to do a lot of things for you."

"You said no romance."

He flashed me a grin. "I'm not being romantic. I'm just trying to get in your pants."

"Is that right?" I asked with a laugh.

The stairwell door closed, and I took his hand, stopping him from walking. I wanted to say something, but my thoughts were muddled with emotions too complicated to express. Too against the rules. Then realizing I didn't want to *say* something, I wanted to *do* something, I leaned in and pressed my lips to his.

The kiss started out so innocent, a little thank-you for rocking my world, but then his free hand slid into my hair and my hands clutched his shirt and suddenly we were pressed against the stairwell door, our bodies flush, every bit of restraint tossed back down the stairs. I had just risen onto my toes for better access to his amazing mouth when a gasp, followed by whispering, sent us flying apart.

My chest heaved as I peered around. A pair of older women scurried down the hall away from us, both their heads shaking in complete disgust. Aidan and I burst out laughing as soon as they rounded the corner, and then he took my hand and led me three doors down to his apartment.

As soon as we stepped inside, I could tell the place was 100 percent Aidan. Dark hardwood floors stretched out from the entryway into a large living room with a fireplace and floor-to-ceiling windows that overlooked the city. The leather couch and dark end tables and art on the wall were all very modern, but then I spied a worn UT blanket folded on the back of the couch.

"We haven't talked about the UT thing. What made you

choose to go there?"

"I grew up in Tennessee, so it was in-state or no education at all."

I twisted around to look at him. "You grew up there? But you don't have an accent."

He smiled. "It rarely comes out to play."

The sun had started to set, giving the sky an orange and red glow, and cueing me in to the time—dinner, then a movie, then...

Aidan walked up behind me and ran his hands down the curve of my waist. "I thought we could order in."

"Sounds perfect." I spun in his arms and rose onto my toes to kiss him again, but he pulled away.

"If you continue to kiss me like that, I won't be able to stop myself, and I know you're hungry."

"I can wait to eat."

His eyes darkened as he peered down at me, his hands gripping my waist, and that look was enough to make me forget eating for a week to stay in bed, doing other things with my mouth, but then my stomach growled, and Aidan's gaze fell to the traitor. "Chinese?"

Aidan went to order the food, while I took the opportunity to look around his apartment. There was only one photo to be seen, in a small five-by-seven wooden frame, the photo inside of a woman, maybe fifty. She was beautiful, her eyes squinted in silent laughter. Instantly, I knew the woman must be his mother. We'd barely talked about her, and I wasn't sure he wanted to. Sometimes talking made it easier to miss someone, but I knew firsthand that talking could also make it worse. Plus, we were already walking a dangerous line. We shared bits of ourselves with the other, yet we claimed this was casual. Nothing about us felt casual.

For the first time all day, the weight of this decision pressed on my chest, fear working its way up my spine. What was I doing here? Four years of focusing on school, two grueling summer internships, all in the name of my career, and here I was jeopardizing it all. The thought released a fresh wave of panic, and I eyed the door. I could stop this right now, say I was sorry, I changed my mind.

But the problem was I hadn't changed my mind.

The war between what I wanted to do and what I *should* do waged on in my mind and heart as I continued on around the room, stopping at a large wooden shelf beside his widescreen. I expected to find it filled with books, but instead records sat in perfectly organized rows. I slid out the first one, then the second, a smile forming on my face. They were all older bands, many of them classic rock. My dad would have loved the collection and loved Aidan for having it.

"I see you've found my other addiction."

I ran a hand across the shelf, my eyes shifting to him. "Other?"

"I thought the first was obvious."

I swallowed hard, every inch of my body acutely aware of how close he stood to me. "I didn't see a record player. Do you listen to them or just collect them?"

Disappearing through a door on the other side of the room, he returned with a record player that appeared to be as old as the records. He set it on the metal coffee table, walked over, and thumbed through the records, then pulled one out and placed it on the player, gently dropping the needle onto the record. I waited, eager to hear what he'd chosen, when the guitar chords for "Sweet Home Alabama" filled the room. I grinned at the nod to my home state and reached for his hand. "Dance with me."

He took my hand and pulled me close, and I expected him to ease us into slow dancing, when he quickly pushed me back out, then rolled me in, so my back was to his chest, our bodies moving in time with the music. My mind drifted back to old line dances back home at the Harvest Festival, haystacks surrounding the dance floor, and the thump of feet keeping time to live music.

Aidan spiraled me back out, then twisted me around again, moving again and again, until we were both laughing, getting more and more into the dance. Suddenly, he tugged me flush against him, his hands sliding down my waist to my legs as we danced, the closeness driving me insane. He gripped my hips and flipped me around, our chests heaving, every thought in my mind on how many pieces of clothing separated us and how long it would take to remove them all. I had just decided to start with his shirt, desperate to see his toned chest again, when a knock sounded from the front door.

"Dammit," I said under my breath, before I could stop myself, and Aidan chuckled.

"I'm learning a lot about you tonight," he said as he went for the door.

"Oh, yeah? Like what?"

He opened the door and took our takeout, then shut it back with a smile on his face. "Are you sure you want to know?"

I went into his kitchen and opened the fridge. "Water or beer?"

His smile widened. "Like that."

"Like what?"

"You're in my refrigerator."

"Am I missing something here?" I eyed the open door, scanning its contents briefly. It was such a guy's fridge, all chaotic and disorganized. I longed to arrange it properly. Line up all the condiments, sort the fruits from the vegetables. The bottled water in a row, then wine, then beer.

Aidan set out the takeout containers on his coffee table. "You've been in my apartment for less than an hour and you're already helping yourself to my kitchen. It's just... different."

I cocked an eyebrow. "Different good or different bad?"

"I like it. And I'll have a beer."

I grabbed the beers and sat down beside him on the couch. "So, I'm listening," I said, reaching for one of the containers without asking which was mine. I settled into his couch and crossed my legs up under me.

He burst out laughing. "Nothing makes you uneasy, does it?"

"Are you joking? There are a thousand things that make me uneasy. One of them is staring at me right now."

"You just seem very comfortable in your skin. Most women smooth their hair or watch their posture or do something they feel looks sexy, but you? You're just you, Cameron, take it or leave it, and I find myself wanting to take every bit that you're willing to offer."

My gaze locked on his as I tried and failed to keep my emotions from rising at his words. Why did he do that? Say things that made me desperate for a future with him, when we couldn't take this further? I had a decision to make, and I could feel the clock ticking toward an unspoken end. Either I do what I came here to do, or I leave. Only I didn't want to leave. I wanted to bring up his parents, ask if he thought he'd ever marry. Ask what he wanted for his future. But I was afraid to hear the answer. I felt myself growing comfortable around him, label or not, and I didn't want to give this up. Not yet.

"What else have you learned?" I set my container on the coffee table and rose onto my knees in front of him.

"You're embarrassed of where you're from, but you love it. I'm not sure you even admit that to yourself. But I could see it when you danced, how free you were. Even if you resent it, you love the South. All of it. The people. The food. The atmosphere. I know, because I love it, too."

I edged closer to him with each word, like an invisible rope drew me in. The room grew warmer, a charge igniting in the air. Sensing the change, he set his container down beside mine.

"What else?"

"You hate to lose control. You're organized to a fault."

Still closer.

"What else?"

"I think you're the most amazing person I've ever met. Maybe the most amazing person I'll ever meet. And I don't want anyone else to know the things I know that make you so amazing. I don't want to risk them seeing what I see and stealing you away."

I straddled his lap, my throat tight. "I hate when you say things like that."

He brushed my hair from my face. "Why?"

"Because it doesn't fit in my head. You say these things, but we have rules. You refuse to commit."

"Do you want a commitment from me?"

"No."

Yes. No. Maybe.

"Then what's the problem?"

"We're risking a lot for this. Both of us. Just…are we making the right decision?"

"No," he said. "But I don't care. The question is, do you?"

I considered the question, my eyes on his, two answers weighing in my mind, but despite what was right in action, only one answer felt right.

"No," I whispered.

"Then I think we're done talking." He focused on my mouth, and as though he couldn't wait another second, his lips gently touched mine, his hands in my hair, and then attraction took over, and the sweet kiss turned intense. It was full of the fears we both felt, the rush and excitement of knowing the risk, but being unable to stay away.

Aidan lifted me up, wrapping my legs around his waist, his lips never leaving mine as he walked across the room and pushed open a door. The room was dark except for a strip of light cascading in from the living room. He set me down just before a king bed and ran his hands over my face, then down to my shirt, tracing the edge, telling me without words that he wanted it off.

I gripped the hem and tugged the shirt over my head, revealing the black lace bra I'd picked out just for this occasion. He glanced down, and the sight of him, so full of want, sent my insides into a spiral. I shimmied out of my leggings and lay back on his bed, enjoying the feel of his gaze on my flesh, then he was over me, his hands skimming my thighs, then my stomach, then my breasts, each smooth touch causing my breathing to speed up. His lips pressed against my collarbone, then the swell of my breast, and my back arched, each second driving me more and more insane. I slid my hands under his shirt, running them over his taut abs, and then the shirt was off, and he kicked out of his jeans, and all the longing we'd had since that first night burst to the surface, overflowing with nothing but need.

He flicked the clasp on my bra and tossed it to the floor with the rest of our clothes, exposing my bare breasts, and then his mouth was on my left nipple, sucking slowly as he rolled his tongue against it, his right hand toying with my other nipple, pulling and pinching, until I screamed out, unable to hold myself back any longer.

My hands clenched his shoulders as he moved back to my mouth, his tongue sweeping inside, taking over, as his hand stroked down my body, slipping inside my panties and gently stroking my core. I bucked against him, my hips lifting on their own accord with each delicious sensation. It'd been so long since I'd allowed my control to slip, my always-thoughtful mind lost to anything but the pleasure of the moment. It was freeing, a high I hadn't felt before, and suddenly I was desperate to test how high I could go.

I slipped my hands into his boxers, running them over his amazing ass, then to his length, and he groaned against my neck. "Cameron…"

"Now."

The sound of fabric ripping filled the air, and then my panties were off, my body fully naked below him. Aidan slipped a finger inside me, his eyes on me, and the intensity in them caused the fire burning in my core to rage out of control. His perfect mouth touched my thigh, gliding up, up, up, and then he took me in his mouth, licking and tasting, until my entire body shook with the need to have him inside me.

"Aidan, please," I begged, not recognizing the desperation in my voice. I'd never needed anything like I needed this release.

In one swift move, his boxers were off, and he reached for a condom from his nightstand. His sudden absence made my body shake with the need for him to return. And then he was back over me, his lips crashing onto mine in a kiss that felt less like a kiss and more like a long, deep breath after being underwater for far too long. We lost all restraint, our hands everywhere, and then he thrust inside me and all I could do was scream out his name, over and over, until my insides felt boneless and utterly content. My body quaked one final time as Aidan released, and then his body relaxed against me, our breaths heavy.

He combed my hair gently as he pulled my back flush against his chest, and I closed my eyes, exhaustion taking over, yet a part of me still wanted more. Would I ever get enough of this man? Memories of our first night together poured in—hot kisses, overwhelming passion—but this was something else. Something more.

"Cameron?"

"Hmm?"

"Stay for the weekend."

I stilled in his arms, sure I hadn't heard him right, then turned around, blinking as I peered up at him. "What did you say?"

"Stay with me for the weekend."

A smile played at my lips, refusing to be contained. "All right." Nuzzling my head under his neck, I drew in his all-manly smell, content that for now I didn't have to worry about our jobs or forever. For now.

Chapter Sixteen

"So, Lucy broke her ankle?" I asked as I lay back on the couch, my legs on Aidan's lap. I'd been on the phone with my mom for twenty minutes, listening to the full family update, and for once, I didn't want to hurry her off the phone. There was something about being here with Aidan and talking to Mom that made it all feel very real. A part of me wanted her to ask where I was, what I was doing here, all so I would have to look at Aidan with my eyebrows lifted, because God, did I ever want to know. What was I doing here?

Hoping.

That was what I was doing. Despite my agreement to follow the rules, I found myself hoping for more. I liked being with him, liked the feel of his warm arms around me.

"What was that?" Mom asked.

"Oh, I didn't say anything."

"Not you. Eric. What? What!" she called out, shattering my eardrum.

"I'm talking to Cammie. What? No. Cam-mie!"

"Mom?"

"No, not Sally. You need to go see Dr. Hand!"

"Mom?"

"There's nothing wrong with hearing aids if you need them!"

"Oh my God. Mom."

"What?"

"You sound busy. Why don't I call you tomorrow?"

I heard a ruffling sound, following by a spraying sound. She was cleaning, likely something that was already clean. "All right then, love. Talk to you tomorrow."

I hung up and set the phone on my stomach, smiling at the ceiling.

"Why was your mom screaming?" Aidan asked as he flicked between two games on the TV.

"Oh, she wasn't. Well, technically she was, but she and Eric like to scream out at the other from across the house. Or across the yard. Or anywhere, really." I smiled again. "It's just one of their things."

Aidan's face hardened. "Yeah, screaming was one of my parents' things, too. Or maybe just my dad."

"Did he yell a lot?"

A commercial flashed across the TV, and both our eyes turned, picking it apart, analyzing, trying to see how we might have done it differently.

"God, that was terrible."

"It's a Graham Group ad," Aidan said with a nod. "He's too traditional. Always has been. But to answer your question—no. He wasn't a yeller. He preferred to make my mom feel like she didn't deserve to be his wife, didn't deserve to even be in his presence. I remember one Halloween we were going to a holiday party at his office. All the kids were supposed to dress up and the offices would each give out candy. Well, I wanted to be a dinosaur, but Mom couldn't find a costume, so she decided to make it. The costume looked like a pickle with teeth, but she was so proud. Until Dad walked in the door. I'll never forget the look on his face when he saw me. Like he'd never been more disgusted in his life. He grabbed my mom by the arm and dragged her up to my room, me crying after them, and started throwing all my clothes out of my closet, ordering her to take that shit off me and put on something presentable. She'd worked for weeks on the costume, only to have him throw it in the trash."

"I'm so sorry."

He shrugged. "It's done. Besides, that was mild."

I thought of what I could say to make him feel better, but our pasts couldn't be erased with kind words in the present. They were a part of us, a living, breathing thing in our lives. I hadn't met Aidan's father, but the more I heard about him, the more I understood why Aidan was afraid to end up like him. Then I realized that with his mother gone and his jerk of a father, he had no one. No family to visit with. No place to go for the holidays.

"Do you have other family?"

Aidan cleared his throat and glanced out the window. "Not really. I'm not close with my extended family."

"But then what do you do over the holidays? Where do you go?"

"I work."

My heart clenched as I watched his face flicker with hurt before he cleared it of any emotion, and I knew the conversation was over.

"Let's grab lunch. We can go somewhere private, outside our norm, no one we know anywhere around." Standing, I reached for his hand, helping him up. Hopefully getting out would pull his mind from his father. "Please?"

"I know just the place."

We started out the door when I glanced over at him, unable to hold my tongue. "You know you would never be that kind of father, right?"

Aidan locked his door and then reached for my hand. "I don't plan to find out."

"What do you mean? You don't want kids?"

"No wife, no kids. Kind of need the first to get the second, right? Stairs?"

A sinking feeling worked through me, refusing to settle. "Yeah…the stairs."

Chapter Seventeen

I started for my cube Monday morning, my mind still on the weekend, when Gayle motioned for me to come to her office. Immediately, my pulse sped up, even though I knew I was being ridiculous. We hadn't left Aidan's apartment except for lunch on Sunday, and surely no one saw me go into his building, right? And even if someone had, I could have been visiting a friend, a relative, anyone. This was nothing. Nothing at all.

So why couldn't I stop shaking?

She motioned for me to close the door, and I sat down in one of the chairs in front of her desk and crossed my legs, then uncrossed them, threaded my fingers, then rested them flat in my lap. My mind was a frazzled mess, and she hadn't even spoken.

"Doing okay this morning?" she asked. She was smiling. That had to mean everything was fine. Everything was absolutely fine. Totally fine. Absolutely, totally fine.

"Sure. How about you?"

She bobbed her head. "Good. So, look, I saw the Blast mock-up this morning. Aidan said you were behind most of it, and I have to tell you, Cameron, it's genius. They'll love it. I know it."

I released a breath. Thank God, this was about work and nothing more. I sat back in my chair, telling my heart it was okay to settle down. No heart attacks on the agenda for today.

"I'm glad you like it. So, you just wanted to talk about the campaign?"

Her face went serious and she leaned in closer. "Well, actually, no." Oh shit, this was it. I swallowed hard and prepared to hear some ultimatum—*if it happens again, you're fired.* Or maybe she would fire me now, cut her losses, and find someone who could work without falling for her boss. Oh my God. Maybe Aidan was in a similar meeting with the partners right now. Shit, shit, shit.

"I called you in here to tell you that you're getting a bonus for coming up with the idea. If Blast takes it, you'll get a five-thousand-dollar bonus and likely be promoted to account executive at the first of the year."

"A bonus. Seriously?" So not the direction I'd envisioned in my head.

"You deserve it. And Aidan seems to really like you. He's very picky, but he's always going on and on about your potential. It pays to get in with the boss." She winked.

My eyes widened. I couldn't tell if she was joking or serious. Either way, we had to be more careful, but how could we be more careful than keeping our relationship to abandoned stairwells and our apartments?

Gayle checked her watch and then stood abruptly. "We better get in there. The meeting's about to begin." I followed her into the conference room, intentionally keeping my eyes in front of me, on the floor, then my chair—anywhere but at the front of the table, to where I knew Aidan sat. Once we were settled, Aidan conference-called Trevor from Blast, and we waited for everyone on his end to arrive.

"All right, then," Aidan said. He started into his presentation, both addressing the Blast Water team and our own, his tone and his movements growing more enthusiastic as he spoke. He loved his job, that much was clear, but it was more than that. This was a challenge to him, and his competitive side needed the win. When he finished talking, he pressed his hands against the table and leaned in closer to the phone. "We believe this campaign can take your brand to the next level with not only college football, but sports in general."

There was silence on the other end, followed by assents and discussion. We waited. I took the opportunity to look at the final mock-up. It had Aidan written all over it, but it was also me. My notes. My details. I stared at the picture of the child on the left and the man on the right, and I wanted the drink in his hand. If that drink turned a kid into a hero, on the field or not, I wanted that drink. In short, it was perfect. I smiled and glanced over at Aidan before I could help myself, only to find him watching me. Our gazes held for a moment, a half second, no more, but the sensation was immediate. My chest became numb and my legs felt weak. I was back there, feeling his firm body against mine, his breath on my neck. I wondered if he was there, too. If we shared this moment of dual realities. And if so, which one did he prefer? His eyes cut away before I could guess.

Finally Trevor broke the silence. "Aidan?"

Aidan focused back on the phone, his face completely at ease, as though we were talking about lunch instead of a multimillion-dollar business deal. "I'm here."

Trevor hesitated, and I fought the urge to tell him to hurry up. After what felt like forever, he finally spoke up. "We love it."

The creative team high-fived and Gayle grabbed my hand. "We did it," she whispered. I smiled back, even though Gayle had next to no input on the mock-up. Aidan straightened, his face lit. "We're glad. We'll begin work immediately."

The call ended, and Aidan clapped his hands together loudly to quiet down our zealousness. "Great work, team. You should be pleased with yourselves." Then he looked at me. "And we should all thank Cameron for her creativity with the idea. She'll run point on the campaign. Cameron, I want your eye on every element of this project. This is your baby. Help her grow."

I nodded and Gayle beamed. She really was an amazing boss. She gave me assignments and supported me, but otherwise stayed out of my hair. The best kind of boss. Aidan started in on a few other campaigns the agency was working on, potential clients, and statistics for one of the latest campaigns, but I barely listened. My body felt light from the excitement, my heart warm from a weekend I couldn't forget.

My phone buzzed as soon as I reached my cube after the meeting, and I picked it up to find a text from my mom asking if I had received my ticket for Thanksgiving. *My what?* I sat down in my chair, woke up my computer, and opened Outlook. Sure enough, three unread emails down from the top sat a flight confirmation. My heart warmed at the sight of it. Thanksgiving was a month away, and I'd assumed that I would spend it in the city, my account too low to support a flight home when I'd already booked one for Christmas. But I missed my family. I missed my mom's muffins in the morning and the smell of coffee all the way up the stairs. I missed how Eric refused to talk to you until he'd finished reading the paper, and how their cat—Sasha—hated everyone but him. Sitting back in my chair, I typed back to Mom: *You're amazing. Thank you! I'll pay you back. Promise!*

After finishing up a few emails, I started down the hall for the bathroom when I felt the presence of someone behind me. I fought to keep the smile from my face as I took in his telltale spicy cologne.

Aidan.

He nodded to a door to the left, a room I'd never been in before, then slipped inside. "Aidan," I whispered after him, but he didn't reply. My pulse sped up as I went on to the women's room, my thoughts everywhere. Surely he wouldn't risk something here, behind closed doors or not, but then why meet there instead of his office if this was work-related? I contemplated ignoring him, the good girl in me freaking out that we could get caught, and even talking in some random room looked suspicious, but then I stepped back into the hall, my eyes on the door. There was no one walking by, so I knocked once, and then when no one answered, glanced down the hall again and whispered his name. Once again he didn't answer. I bit my lip, my stomach in knots, but then I thought of Aidan inside, waiting for me, and the worry was replaced with excitement.

I pushed open the door. It closed quickly but quietly behind me to expose a small meeting room with nothing more than a tiny round table, three chairs around it, and a desk with a computer on it in the far left side. A few boxes were stacked here and there that appeared to have found their final resting place. The room looked like it had once been someone's office and was now used primarily for storage.

I turned toward Aidan, prepared to ask him what he was doing, when he placed a finger to his lips and pulled me against him, his mouth on mine before I could say another word. Mixing the Aidan I knew out of the office with Aidan, my boss, became too much, and before I could control myself, my hands were in his hair, tugging him closer, my insides awakening, begging for a repeat from the weekend.

His hands slid down my back, gripping my backside, and all I could think about was the table and whether it could support our weight. I had just decided that I was willing to take the chance when the doorknob to the room jiggled. And then the jiggling became knocking.

Oh, crap.

I jumped away from Aidan, my heart hammering away in my chest. This was it. We'd been officially together for one weekend, and now it was over. Fired. I tried to tell myself to calm down. We hadn't been caught doing anything. We were just in an abandoned storage room. Alone. In the dark.

Forget *oh crap*, this was a full-out *fucked*.

Aidan took my hand and raised it to his lips, kissing my palm easily, his entire demeanor the very definition of calm. He mouthed that it was okay and pointed to a small door beside the desk. I mouthed back *closet* and he nodded. I shook my head. There was no way I could close myself inside a tiny closet without a complete claustrophobic melt-down. But this was my job on the line, and if things got bad,

I could just open the door.

"Is someone in there?" a voice called from outside the door, and suddenly all the blood drained from my face, the fear of losing my job greater than the fear of suffocating. Drawing a deep breath, I opened the closet and tucked myself inside, my hand ready on the knob.

My pulse sped up as my breathing became labored, thoughts rushing through one after the other. He knew I hated small spaces; he knew what this would do to me. Anger burned through me as I listened for movement outside the door, my head throbbing now from the effort to stay quiet, to control my breathing—to keep from shouting at Aidan through the door for making me do this. Only, he wasn't making me do anything at all. I had walked into this room. I had stepped into the closet. I had closed the door. And now my anger turned on myself, which made me all the more irritated at him.

Aidan opened the door to the room, and then his administrative assistant's voice filled the silence. They spoke for a second, and I tried not to make a sound, not to breathe, not to exist.

I waited until there were no more voices and then slipped out of the closet to find an empty room. Aidan must have left with Dorothy, giving me the clear to leave without anyone seeing.

Reaching my cube, I pulled out my phone and texted Aidan.

What was that? We agreed to nothing on our floor, you break it, and then I'm stuck in my worst nightmare?

Immediately, a text popped up with, *I'm sorry. You're right. I shouldn't have taken the chance.*

This is my job. I can't take risks like this. I'm not you. I don't have the stability you have.

My phone went dark as seconds turned into a minute, and I had to suppress the urge to text again ordering him to hurry up with his reply, so I could text-yell at him some more. Then it vibrated with, *I said I was sorry , and you're not the only one taking a risk. And I'm sorry about the closet.*

My anger dissipated as I realized he was right. I wasn't the only one taking a risk. He was in this, too, and it wasn't like he forced me to follow. I'd made the decision.

I'm sorry. It wasn't fair to yell at you.

Aidan: *No, you're right. I shouldn't have taken the risk. Can I make it up to you?*

I thought of our time together that weekend, how great it felt to be with him without worrying that someone might see. And then I remembered the conversation we had about his lack of family, him working over the holidays because he had nothing else to do. A thought occurred to me.

Come home with me for Thanksgiving.

I couldn't imagine him here, all alone, while I was back home, laughing with my family, stuffing myself with Mom's amazing turkey and dressing.

Aidan: *We said no family or friends.*

We also said nothing on our floor.

Aidan: *You don't play fair.*

Is that a yes?

Rising up to peer over my cube, I saw Aidan pick up his phone, then his head turned and his gaze locked on mine. I thought maybe he'd say no, that he'd say it was too much, we weren't serious. But then a grin broke across his face and my phone pinged with a new text, his eyes never leaving mine.

All right, but I think we need a new set of rules.

Chapter Eighteen

Our flight landed in Birmingham at just after two the day before Thanksgiving. Two antianxiety pills, a new book on my Kindle, and Aidan's hand in mine kept my nerves in check so I could fly without my claustrophobia sending me into fits. Thankfully, I had a few days on the ground before I had to repeat it all over again to return back home.

I half expected Mom to have sent one of my cousins, her baking away at home, but then I saw her there, her eyes filling with tears. She rushed up to me and I let her hug me too tight and kiss each of my cheeks with her bloodred lipstick. Only my mother would put on lipstick just to go to the airport. Like always, her blond hair was cut into a shaggy bob, à la Meg Ryan. She refused to try a different style, and I had long since learned to stop asking her. Eric smiled over at me. My stepdad was nearly six five and built like a lineman. For an old man, he was as intimidating as they came.

"How was the flight?" He didn't try to hug me. Eric had

been my father figure for more years than my actual father, but he refused to push. He waited for me to come to him, something I had always respected about him. But before I could hug him, his eyes traveled past me, and he straightened, protective father taking over. They knew Aidan was coming, but knowing wasn't the same as seeing him here.

Mom pulled away from me, noticing Aidan standing behind me. He'd remained a few steps back, allowing us to have our reunion in private. But now, my parents' eyes were both on him, Mom's full of intrigue, Eric's uneasy.

"Mom, Eric, this is Aidan. He's a friend of mine from work." We'd decided to keep the boss thing to ourselves for now, sure it would only complicate things, and besides, they wouldn't see him again, so what did it matter?

Mom blinked away her questioning expression, then broke into her telltale charismatic self. Aidan reached out a hand to her, but Mom was a hugger all the way and instead wrapped her arms around him and squeezed lightly before stepping away. "We're so glad to have you here."

"It's a pleasure to meet you, Mrs. Lawson. Cameron talks about you all the time."

Mom eyed me, clearly curious what the story was between Aidan and me. "Paterson, actually."

"Oh, I…" Aidan turned to me. "I'm sorry. Of course Lawson would be…"

Mom waved a hand through the air. "Don't fret. And please, call me Lorelei."

I smiled reassuringly to him, wishing I had remembered to mention that my mother's last name wasn't the same as mine, but relieved all the same to see the tension relaxing from around his eyes. As crazy as my family could get, we were still a family, and Aidan shouldn't have to miss out on a traditional Thanksgiving celebration just because his father was a jerk.

"Well, let's get on," Eric said. "Your aunts will be over any minute now to 'help.'"

"When are you going to leave them alone?" Mom said, and they settled into one of their arguments about my mom's sisters, her claiming they had good intentions, and Eric claiming they came over just to gossip. (He was right.)

I grinned as I listened, and then noticed Mom veer toward a black Tahoe. Not at all the old red truck Eric had for most of my childhood. "Don't tell me she forced you to get rid of Judith?" Eric liked to name his cars old-woman names. I used to tell him he should choose something hot like Candy, but he said he wanted something dependable, and women named Candy were anything but dependable.

He sighed. "She broke down once, and that was the end of it. Your mother refused to ride in Judith again, which might sound nice, except I like her to keep me company on occasion."

I smiled at Mom. "So you bought a Tahoe so Mom would keep you company? How romantic."

Eric shrugged. "I'll be alone when I'm dead, and there are very few people I like. What can I say? I prefer to keep the people I like close."

"Alone when you're dead, huh? Better not tell Pastor Wilkins you said that."

He laughed. "Yeah, well, it'll be our little secret."

Aidan placed our bags in the back of the Tahoe and opened my door, earning a grin from Mom. Then she slipped into the seat beside me. "You sit up front, Aidan. Stretch those long legs."

She winked at me as he took his seat beside Eric, both men's postures so tight I wondered if I'd made a terrible decision throwing him on them like this. Eric started down the highway, and Mom clapped her hands. "Well, now, let's see. What have you missed? Lexie just had twins, but there are rumors the father is in question. They'd been having trouble, you see. Trudy said they went to that fancy in vitro doctor in Atlanta. Then poof, she's pregnant. With twins! I don't know. Jack sure travels a lot. It's possible, but Trudy wouldn't breathe a word about it if it were true. You know she's all about image."

Trudy was Mom's eldest sister, and Lexie was one of my cousins, so both would be at our house for Thanksgiving.

"Mom, it's not uncommon for those who get in vitro to become pregnant with multiples. I'm sure that's what happened. Y'all need to stop gossiping so much." And there it was—*y'all*. It was like coming back to the South put an injection of Southern lingo straight into my brain. *Welcome home, here you go. Here's some good ole Southern-speak. You'll be right as rain.*

I caught Eric's gaze from the rearview mirror. He was silently warning me. Mom was volatile on a good day. She cried or yelled at a moment's notice. Eric and I had learned not to push her buttons. Or mention that she took Prozac. God forbid.

Forcing a smile on my face, I switched subjects. "Tell me about Madison and Emma." Maddie and Emma were sisters and the only two cousins I actually liked, partially because they were both wonderful, but also because they were outcasts like me. Maddie had come out sometime around senior year of high school and had been in a committed relationship ever since. And Emma was married to a short black man. I still wasn't sure what offended her mother more—that Jayden was black or that he was short. But he was an amazing husband, and truly, that's all that should matter.

Mom shook her head. "Well, about the same. Poor Beth is beside herself, but what can she do? We can only do so much for our children." She peered over at me as if to say, *yep, look how you turned out*. Fantastic. But then her gaze switched up to Aidan and her face changed, a hint of something there that wasn't before. Like curiosity or maybe hope, and I wished I could dispel her hope for a June wedding right now. Whatever this was, it wasn't *that*.

I pulled my phone from my bag, telling myself that I was going to check the time and shove it back into its spot in my purse, but I couldn't stop myself from checking my text messages. A smile spread across my face as I read the latest message.

Aidan: *Did I mention that you look amazing today?*

My heart swelled until I realized that Mom had stopped talking and was reading over my shoulder. Her eyes brightened as she peered up at me, then she settled into her seat, her gaze out her window, a warm smile on her face.

We reached our long driveway, and I grinned at the sight of our large white Victorian-style home. The house had been my great-grandparents' and held all the bangs and bruises of an old house. The roof leaked no matter how often they had it fixed. The water took forever to heat up. And at night you could almost always hear some animal scurrying in the attic.

Still, it was home, and seeing it after all these months made my heart happy.

Eric parked in the detached garage he'd built years ago. He and Aidan had barely spoken, and I wondered what was causing the issue.

Maybe his age. Maybe he sensed that we were hiding something. Or maybe it all had to do with Aidan being male and me being his daughter. I'd only ever brought Blaine home to meet my parents, and he'd grown up in Birmingham, like me. There was something reassuring about knowing what a person looked like in diapers. It made them less intimidating—less of a threat. That had to be it. They'd never seen Aidan in diapers.

The thought made me giggle, and he poked my side as we walked up the steps to our wraparound front porch. "What?"

"Nothing. Just…you're unexpected."

He tucked a loose strand of hair behind my ear. "So are you."

A smile played at my lips as I peered back up, only to find Mom in the doorway, watching our exchange.

"I'm so glad you're here, Aidan," she said, her eyes shiny.

"I'm glad to be here, Mrs. Paterson."

"Lorelei."

"Lorelei."

"Well, why don't you show him around, Cammie? Then maybe he could help Eric cut some firewood, while you help me in the kitchen?"

My eyes widened at Aidan. "Um…"

"I'd love to help," he assured me, then her. "Wherever you need me."

By some miracle my extended family had not arrived yet, so with Mom off in the kitchen and Eric outside, I led Aidan upstairs to my room and showed him the guest room beside my room, where my parents would expect him to sleep.

"Where's their room?"

"Downstairs."

"So," Aidan asked, pulling me into his arms and gently trailing kisses from my neck to my ear and back, "if I were to sneak into your room, they wouldn't notice?"

"Naughty."

He caught my earlobe between his teeth and whispered, "With any luck."

We came down to the sound of Mom humming in the kitchen and the crackle of a fire from the fireplace in the great room. Contentment settled over me as I opened the back door to our deck, the small lake behind our house glistening in the afternoon sun. The woods surrounding it were all painted in the yellows and oranges and reds of fall, except for the evergreen pines. I smiled fondly at memories out on our dock, my legs hanging over the side as Eric cast from beside me, then when he caught something, I'd jump up and he'd pass me the rod, allowing me to reel it in. Like I'd caught the fish instead of him.

The deck led to a flagstone patio, complete with a stone fire pit and matching stone grill. A glass table with four chairs around it sat untouched.

I pointed to the swing hanging under the deck, just beside the spa. "That's the swing Eric proposed to my mom on. It was in one of the gardens in town, and he convinced them to let him replace it with a new one, so he could have that one. It was rotting at the time, but he restored it and hung it here. Mom gets goose bumps every time she sits on it, like it takes her right back to that day."

"Now, you're going to make him think I'm a romantic," Eric called from beside the old barn he converted into a work area years ago.

"You are a romantic."

Eric started to argue, then shrugged. "I have my moments. Chain saw or splitting maul, Aidan?" he asked.

"I can split 'em," Aidan said, and I couldn't help grinning as his accent returned.

"Good."

Aidan pushed up the sleeves of his waffle shirt and gripped the ax, causing me to dive into fantasies of him getting especially worked up and having to remove that shirt and—

"Cammie!" Mom called from the porch. "Need you!"

I waved apologetically to Aidan. "I'll bring you some drinks out in a bit."

Walking away, I heard Eric ask Aidan where he'd graduated, and then a grin spread across my face as Aidan said Tennessee, and they settled into talk of football and the SEC and who might end up in the title game this year.

Once back inside, I found Mom kneading dough, her phone tucked between her chin and shoulder. "No, we're good today. Yes, I'm sure. Yes, just come tomorrow morning. Yes, eating at one like always. Yes, right. Yes, one. Cammie's here. No, Eric's fine. She brought a friend." She nodded to a bowl of peaches and then the knife and cutting board in front of them. I went to work. "I don't know. Just a friend. Maybe more." Her eyebrows rose at me in question, and I shook my head with a laugh.

But then it occurred to me that Aidan and I could never be more. Not really. He would never want a commitment, would never spend another Thanksgiving with me. I knew what I was getting into with him, yet I wanted more.

I focused back on the peaches, telling myself I would talk to him when we returned to New York. The rules became more muddled the more time we spent together, so why not ask about our future? Why not want more? And maybe he would be happy. Maybe he would agree and kiss me and say he didn't want this to end.

My gaze drifted out into the kitchen, my nerves coiling tighter with each disillusioned thought. Because despite all the maybes, deep down I knew he was far more likely to kiss my cheek and leave.

Chapter Nineteen

I came outside an hour later to check on Aidan and Eric to find them laughing, both men covered in sweat despite the November chill. Aidan had shed his waffle shirt to just a fitted white undershirt and low-hanging jeans, and suddenly that fantasy from before came roaring back to life.

"Water?" I asked, holding out two cold bottles.

Eric grabbed his. "Thanks." He took a long sip, then clapped Aidan on the back. "I need to go make a call. Be back in a bit." He winked over at me before disappearing through the basement door into their finished basement—aka Eric's man cave.

I gripped the ax and spread my legs out. "All right. Tell me what to hit."

Aidan laughed. "Settle down there before you hurt somebody."

"Hey, now. I can do it."

He unscrewed his water and took a long pull, then set a

log up for me. "All right, then, Ms. Mighty. Go right ahead. Just let me step back a few yards."

"Funny thing, aren't you?" I said with a glare, then gripping the handle, I lifted it high and brought it down on the log, but it lodged into the wood instead of actually splitting it. Struggling to free the ax, I put my foot on the log and tugged and pulled and yanked, all to no avail, only to glance over to find Aidan in near hysterics.

"Teach you to try to do man's work."

"Man's work? I've got this. I was just playing around before." I fought the ax more before finally growing frustrated and tossing it down, the log still stuck to it like I'd glued them together. "I'm just gonna let that rest for a bit."

"Are you now?" He placed his foot on the log and took the ax in his left hand, jerking it free, then tossed it to the ground. "You're cute, you know that?"

I walked over and draped my arms around his neck. "Cute, huh? Is this cute?" Rising onto my toes, I pressed my lips to his, tempting his mouth open with my tongue and sweeping in to show him just how uncute I could be. Then before my teasing turned to passion, I pulled away and bit my bottom lip.

"I retract previous statement," he said. "No cuteness at all here, folks."

"Come on, let's go down to the dock."

The sun shone from just over the trees now, making everything beautiful. Not a cloud dotted the sky, and I made a mental note to come sit out on the patio tonight to see the stars. We reached the end of the dock and sat down, draping our legs over the side.

"It must have been amazing growing up here."

I thought of the fireworks on the Fourth of July. The family reunions in our backyard. "It was." Then glancing at him, I asked, "Do you have any fond memories from childhood? After your father left, maybe?"

He hesitated, thinking, then gripping the dock and leaning forward to look into the water, he said, "I have a lot of good memories after he left. It's odd. We never wanted for anything when he was there, yet I never felt like I had anything. Never felt content or safe, the way you should in your house. Then he left, and Mom and me had nothing. No money. Shit food. No fancy toys at Christmas. Yet I never missed those things. We were happy."

"What was your favorite memory?"

"When I was twelve I asked for my own bicycle so I could ride to the park for my baseball games instead of walking. It was Christmas, and I'd long since stopped believing in any jolly old man coming to bring me my wishes, but still, there was that hint of kid hope. That anticipation that maybe I'd get lucky and I'd get my wish. And then I woke Christmas morning and came out of my bedroom to find a bike under our tree. It was used and had rust spots, but there it was. Mom made us pancakes and we just stared at that bike, happy for the first time in a long time. That was a good day."

I threaded my fingers through his, running my thumb over his palm. "It sounds like she was a special woman."

"She was. She died too young. Heart disease."

"I'm sorry."

Aidan shrugged and stood, reaching for my hand. "Care if I go in for a shower?"

"Not at all."

I showed him to the bathroom between our two rooms and where to find towels and anything else he might need, then stepped up to kiss him once more, our bodies touching, heat radiating off him in waves. "You smell good," I said, causing him to laugh.

"I smell like sweat."

"You smell like the outdoors. It's nice."

He dipped his head to press his lips to mine, then pulled away. "You better get out of here before I drag you into the shower with me."

Grinning, I went for the door. "We'll have dinner ready when you come back down."

"Royalty treatment. I could get used to this."

I closed the door and leaned against it, smiling. "Yeah… me, too."

. . .

I made my way into the kitchen to help Mom with dinner. The smell of rosemary and spice filled the air, bringing with it a thousand memories of me up on a small wooden stool, bright-eyed as I watched Mom work her magic in the kitchen. She taught me how to bake, how to season, how to make cookies from scratch and the most perfectly moist turkey on the planet. I thought of Grace and Lauren, both of whom couldn't boil water, and felt a surge of pride for all Mom had given me. "Thanks for teaching me to cook," I said as I sorted cheese and bread on the serving tray she'd set out.

"I'd have liked to show you more. I wish you were home so I could."

Sadness and guilt weighed on me. "I know. But I'm

happy in New York."

"I can see that," she said, smiling over at me. "He's nice. Where is his family for the holiday?"

"He lost his mother a few years ago," I said. "That's why I invited him. He would've been alone."

Mom glanced at the doorway to the kitchen, likely listening for Aidan. "What about his dad?"

"Left when he was a kid."

She covered her mouth. "He doesn't have parents?"

"He doesn't have anyone. No family."

She shook her head, her eyebrows drawn in concern. "Well, then, he can share yours."

I pulled her into a hug. "I love you. Thank you."

Mom and I carried the roast and sides into the dining room, where Aidan and Eric sat talking football again. The table brimmed with candles and swirling pumpkin-and-leaf decorations, the perfect holiday centerpiece. I sat down beside Aidan, Mom across from me, and Eric at the head of the table. Mom's best fine china, sterling, and crystal were positioned in place settings in front of us.

Eric stood as soon as we were all seated. "Let us thank God," he said, as he bowed his head. I peeked over at Aidan, expecting him to blanch at the idea of prayer. I'd never once heard him talk about religion. But he had already closed his eyes. "Lord, we thank you for the wonders you give us each day and the blessings that carry us. We thank you for our family, for our health, and for the gift of great friends, like Aidan. We hope to see more of him. In Jesus' name, amen."

I swallowed hard as I opened my eyes and peered at Eric, but he refused to meet my gaze. Aidan was the first guy I had brought home since Blaine. They knew how badly that breakup had hurt me, how hard it was to talk about Blaine for months after. I could only imagine what was going through their heads right now.

"Let's eat."

We took turns passing around dishes and piling our plates to the rims. It made me excited for Thanksgiving. I missed homemade food, how wonderful it smelled, and by the look on Aidan's face, he was thinking the same.

"So, Aidan," Mom said after a few minutes of silent eating. "How exactly did you and Cameron meet?"

Aidan took a drink of his water and wiped his mouth with his napkin before replying. "Well, as Cameron mentioned, we work together. Though we met before she started at Sanderson-Lowe."

"What a nice coincidence."

A smile stretched across my face at the memory, and Aidan grinned at me.

"What do you do at Sanderson-Lowe?" Mom pressed. "Are you an account manager, like Cammie?"

And here it was. The topic we had debated over and over on the plane. Should we admit that Aidan was my boss and deal with the looks now, or skate over it and act as though he were promoted or something later?

Aidan sat tall. "Actually, I'm the chief creative director."

Mom's eyebrows shot up. "That sounds rather important."

He shrugged. "I think every position is important. We operate as a team. One missing piece and everything falls apart."

Eric nodded, the businessman in him showing. "I like your philosophy. I used to tell my employees that every person on my staff needs to be prepared to sweep the floor if necessary."

"Exactly," Aidan said, and just like that, their conversation shifted from football to business, and I watched with pride as Eric listened to Aidan talk. I'd seen Aidan captivate a room plenty of times at the office. To see him do the same to Eric, someone I'd always respected, made my heart swell. When I glanced up, I found Mom's eyes on me, tears threatening to rain.

"Are you all right?" I asked.

"I'm perfect." She reached across for my hand and held it tight. "It's just nice to see you so happy."

After dinner, Mom made an effort of appearing wide-awake so we could have tea and chat, but I knew her too well to allow it. She'd been up since four preparing for Thanksgiving and would be up again tomorrow at four. She needed rest. Plus, I was eager to have Aidan alone.

Aidan disappeared into the guest room, shutting the door with a devilish grin. I went into my room, set my bag on my bed, and clicked on the lamp. Mom had replaced my bedding with a plaid and floral set, but outside of that singular switch, it hadn't changed a bit. The white shelves across from my bed were still full of photos from high school, trophies from competition cheerleading and dance, old baseball cards that I'd collected with my dad. On the nightstand beside the bed sat a porcelain jewelry holder and a framed photo of me sitting in my dad's lap. I was five or six and so scrawny you'd have thought they never fed me, but the smile on my face told the true story. I didn't remember that day. Not where we were, or what we were doing, or even why I was smiling, but I knew that since his death, I never smiled that big.

Except when I was with Aidan.

My thoughts went to the weekend we'd spent at his apartment. Of dancing to "Sweet Home Alabama," him spinning me all around, my body buzzing with such intense happiness that I hardly recognized the feeling. And now him here, in my world, everything feeling so perfect that I didn't want us to leave, to return to the complications of our situation. To have the conversation I knew we needed to have.

Sitting down on my bed, already in fresh pajamas, I heard a soft knock on the door to the bathroom we shared. I walked over and opened it, expecting a joke about getting our naughty on, but the expression on his face made my smile disappear. "What's wrong?"

He reached out to take my hand, gliding our fingers together, watching the way they fit. My small hands into his larger ones. "My father had a heart attack."

"Oh my God. Do you need to fly out? Make a call? What can we do?"

He shook his head and started into my room, lying back on my bed without asking, and despite the situation, I thought of the first time I'd been in his apartment. How he'd noted my helping myself to the refrigerator. It was nice that he felt equally comfortable with me.

"Nothing," he said finally. "His assistant left me a message. She said he's all right, it's just…"

"Aidan?" He peered over at me, his eyes full of anguish. "It's okay to care about him."

"He has never once in his life given a damn about me. Didn't even bother to come to the hospital or funeral when Mom died. So why should I care about him?"

I sat down beside him and ran my fingers through his

hair, then over his forehead, soothing the tension in his brow. "It's not whether you should. You do. He's your father, good or bad, and your caring for him doesn't make you weak. It makes you strong."

"You think so?"

"I do."

We fell into silence then, him staring at the ceiling, me staring at him, before he patted the space beside him and said, "Lie with me."

"But your dad. Do you want to—"

"Please…just lie with me."

Doing as he asked, I lay down beside him, nestling my head under his chin, wishing I knew what he was thinking. Wishing he would talk about it. But sometimes we needed to sort out our thoughts in silence, the quiet giving way to understanding in a way words never could.

"I'm here," I said. He nodded once and then we settled against each other, our eyelids closing somewhere along the way, our bodies tangled together as we drifted into a peaceful sleep.

Chapter Twenty

The sounds of complete and utter chaos startled me awake. I glanced over at the clock on my nightstand and groaned. Seven a.m.

And so it began.

My aunts would arrive soon, bringing with them stress and noise, driving Mom to drink. I needed to get up to help, but instead, I snuggled into Aidan, burying my face in his chest, telling myself I'd get up in five minutes. With any luck, maybe they hadn't arrived.

Thanksgiving never used to be this stressful. Or maybe that was just childhood ignorance, and it had always been stressful for Mom. She used to cook the full meal, and everyone came over about an hour before to "help," which really meant to watch her cook while they talked. But then Dad died, and everything in our lives broke a little. That first Thanksgiving was the hardest, and being from a huge family like ours made it even harder. Mom sat in a corner throughout the whole thing, my aunts busily making the Thanksgiving meal. She didn't cry, but she didn't speak either, which for my mom was worse than crying. It meant she was too lost to do anything, to talk—to feel. But then the second year came, and the third, then she met Eric, and though a part of me resented her for moving on, the rest of me was just happy to see life in her eyes again.

I had just leaned over to give Aidan a quick kiss before slipping into the shower when a sudden pounding on my bedroom door made me freeze midmotion. Hesitating, I stared at the door. Maybe I could ignore it and they'd just—

Bang, bang, bang, bang, bang.

"Cammie, I know you're awake, and if you aren't, you should be. We have an emergency."

I recognized the deep Southern drawl of Anna Beth, the eldest of my cousins, and had to suppress the urge to roll my eyes. Her idea of an emergency could be anything from a broken nail to a house fire. I opened the door just as her fist rose to pound again. She was dressed in a khaki corduroy skirt and button-down blouse, with simple brown ballet flats. I ran a mental check of my pajamas—an old Rolling Stones T-shirt that was so big it hung off one shoulder and bright pink flannel pants. Awesome.

"What can I do for you, Anna Beth?"

Her eyes narrowed, then drifted beyond me to my bed, her lips curved into a catlike grin. "I see I'm interrupting something. I can just tell your mama that you're busy. She was needing you downstairs, but clearly—"

"It's fine, I just need to take a quick shower, and I'll—"

Anna Beth cleared her throat and smiled sweetly. "If you had gotten up and dressed like every other adult in this house, you would already be showered. As it sits, she asked for you to come downstairs. Now."

I gritted my teeth together to keep from spitting out a sarcastic response. Anna Beth might not be my favorite cousin, but she was family, and there was a certain protocol for dealing with family. Even the annoying ones who made you want to double-check the bloodline to ensure you were indeed related. "Fine," I said with a sigh. "Lead the way."

I followed Anna Beth down the stairs and into the kitchen, where sure enough, there was an emergency. It looked like flour had waged war on our kitchen, on the counters, on the walls, everywhere. Mom's hands shook as she peered around at the mess.

"Cammie…" Her voice rattled.

"It's all right, Mom. I've got it." My eyes scanned around for a broom and dustpan and landed on a tiny boy in the corner, so covered in flour I couldn't make out which one of my cousins he belonged to. "It's all right," I repeated to him this time. "Go find your mom and get cleaned up, okay?"

He nodded and took off like I'd just freed him from jail, and I went to work cleaning up the flour blizzard that had struck our kitchen.

"How am I am going to make the cobbler without flour?" Mom asked, her hands on her hips.

"I'll go to the store. No big deal."

Her eyes watered. "See, this is why I need you home. You fix things. No one around here knows how to fix anything."

I laughed. "Mom. I'm just cleaning up. It's no big deal."

"It's a huge deal. If you weren't here, we'd all be staring at this mess, wringing our hands, wondering what to do."

"It's fine, really. I almost have this cleaned up, then you

can go back to cooking, and I'll head to the store. All right?"

She pulled me into a hug and began to sob. "Mom. Please. It's okay."

Finally, Eric came in and took Mom out of my arms and told me where to find his keys. I wanted to get showered up, but Mom was already so upset. I didn't want to cause another meltdown by taking too long, and I had no idea how long the cobbler would take to cook. So instead, I darted upstairs and changed my pajama pants for jeans and tossed my hair into a ponytail, then raced back down to find Aidan standing beside the front door, freshly showered and wearing dark jeans and an ivory pullover that set off the golden tones in his skin so perfectly he looked like an angel sent down to guide me through the crazy. Or at least drive me to the store.

"We have an emergency."

"I heard," he said, brushing flour from the tip of my nose. "Where do you need me?" he asked, now for the second time, making my heart warm.

I reached for his hand. "Right with me."

Parking outside the closest grocery store, I bolted inside with Aidan without thinking to check my reflection in the mirror. But it was Thanksgiving Day, and the store was only open until noon. No one would be out. Hopefully. Else Pastor Wilkins might call my parents and claim I needed an intervention. We rushed inside and separated, Aidan saying he wanted to grab some Advil while I found the flour. I began reading the aisle headers in search of it when I heard my name called from behind.

Crap.

I spun around, prepared to give a quick hello-I'm-in-a-hurry sort of greeting, when my gaze locked on the one person I'd prayed I wouldn't see. Blaine.

My mouth gaped as my brain searched for a reply. He looked exactly like I remembered. Wavy brown hair, deep green eyes, the sort of smile of orthodontists' dreams. I glanced down at my wrinkled jeans and Rolling Stones T-shirt. Dear God, this wasn't happening.

"Hey," I managed to say, because the only other option was to run from the store, but then I wouldn't have the damn flour, and this horror would all be for nothing.

He smiled, his gaze drifting down my clothes before returning to my face. "I'm guessing you're at home for Thanksgiving?"

"Guilty." I tried to laugh, but it sounded more like a strangled cough. Just then a brunette walked up to him, her eyes drifting from me to Blaine in question.

"Oh, sorry. Kristin, this is Cameron."

Ah, Kristin. The fiancée. We were only broken up for six months before I was replaced. Three months later they were engaged. It was like something out of a cheesy romantic comedy. Or a horror film.

She looked at me, and then realization hit her and her smile turned tight. "Right. It's nice to meet you." She took in my outfit as Blaine had and I could tell it took effort for her to keep from grimacing. Well, there went the last bit of my dignity.

"Got it!"

I spun as Aidan came out of the aisle, flour in one hand, Advil in the other. "Hey! Aidan! This is Blaine and Kristin!" Why was I speaking in shrill? There should be rules against this kind of encounter. Like check-ins at the entrance. No ex-boyfriends allowed.

Aidan looked quizzically at me, then reached out a hand. "Nice to meet you."

We stood in awkward silence for a beat, rocking on our heels, no one sure of what to say next, when finally I tapped the flour. "Um, we have a flour situation back at the house, so we better…" I motioned toward the register, and Blaine nodded.

"Right. Of course. Well…it was nice seeing you."

I took him in once more. "You, too."

"Ex?" Aidan asked as we slipped back into the car and started back to my house.

I nodded. "*The* ex. Four years together."

Aidan went quiet.

"He broke it off senior year, then nine months later he and Kristin were together and engaged."

"So they were together before?"

Shrugging, I went on. "Maybe. He's a good guy, though. I don't think he would have cheated. Who knows. I guess it doesn't matter now."

"Do you still love him?"

The question caught me off guard. Aidan and I never talked about our romantic pasts. I had no idea if he'd ever had a serious girlfriend, though with his issues with his father I doubted it.

"I'm not sure I ever did, which was maybe part of the problem. We didn't love each other. Not like you should to make a relationship work. Certainly not enough for marriage."

"What about before him?"

I swallowed, thinking back to high school. "Kyle Black. We were together a year. He played football and I cheered.

It was very high school."

We stopped at a traffic light and he looked over, his expression unreadable. "You've only ever had serious relationships?"

I shrugged again. "I like the idea of forever." At this I met his gaze, unwilling to be ashamed of what I wanted in life. Whatever we were didn't change my hopes for my future. But I had to ask. "You've never had one?"

The light turned green. "I've never wanted one."

"Right."

A part of me wanted to ask more, see if he'd ever met someone who tested his resolve. Tell him he was nothing like his father, surely he was his mother made over, but how could I say any of those things? I knew I walked a dangerous line here, my mind and my heart arguing over how to handle this relationship, and I knew somewhere deep in the shadows of my heart I thought I could change his mind. This, us, could change his mind.

Likely, a hundred girls before me had thought the very same thing, and I wondered how many hearts he'd broken along the way, him never offering anything but the truth, the foolish girl hoping for things he would never give.

What was I thinking, inviting him? Bringing a guy home was serious stuff, not something you did with someone who blatantly said he didn't want a future. I thought of Mom and Eric, how much they both seemed to like him, and how hard it would be to explain why he would never show up here again. Drawing a long breath, I stared out my window, my heart heavy.

I never should have invited Aidan home.

• • •

The Thanksgiving meal at my house was like a choreo-graphed dance—plates brought out, then silver, then plat-ters of food, and before long we were all seated at one of six tables decorated around the house. Mom introduced Aidan to the family with pride. They smiled and nodded and asked the normal questions, but otherwise, Thanksgiving flowed like always, and a part of me wondered what it would be like if I lived here. The idea had once been repulsive to me, but now...I didn't know. I found myself missing home.

After eating dessert, we all went outside, and the men threw around a football with the kids, while the women watched with glasses of tea or wine.

"He's very nice," Mom said from beside me. It was the second time she'd complimented him, and I couldn't help feel-ing a surge of relief. I had hoped my family would see Aidan the way I saw him, that they would push aside that controlled persona he put out and see him for the caring, sweet, intelli-gent man that he was inside. That my mom, the person I cared about most, liked Aidan meant the world to me.

I watched Aidan fake a tackle and fall to the ground as three of my cousins' children jumped on him, screaming with delight. "He is," I said finally, wishing every Thanksgiving could be like this.

"Maybe he could join us for Christmas, too?"

My back went rigid. Christmas. I didn't allow myself to think that far ahead when it came to Aidan and me. I liked being with him too much to think ahead.

I opened my mouth to tell her he had to work, when she

called out, "Aidan?"

"Mom, no. Let me—"

"Nonsense."

He jogged over, his hair sticking out in a thousand directions, bits of grass and leaves mixed in like he'd rolled around all day in the yard. I picked out a leaf, smiling.

"Nice."

"Oh, you like that, do you? We have a volunteer!"

Then he scooped me up and carried me across the yard, holding me down as the kids covered me in leaves. Finally, he released me and helped me to my feet, plucking leaves from my hair as he laughed. Then his eyes met mine and he leaned down to kiss me, ignoring my family. Like it was just the two of us under the clear blue sky.

We walked back to the patio, my thoughts muddled, my chest warm. I'd completely forgotten about what Mom wanted to ask him until Aidan said, "Sorry, Lorelei. What were you saying?"

Her grin spread. "I wanted to invite you to spend Christmas with us."

He hesitated as his gaze drifted from Mom to me. "Oh...I wouldn't want to intrude."

"No intrusion at all. We would love to have you."

My throat constricted as Aidan flashed her a tight smile. "Sure. Count me in."

Chapter Twenty-One

Aidan closed the door to his apartment the next day, set my bag on the couch, and turned around to face me. We'd barely spoken on the plane, and now that we were alone, I felt the full weight of the tension that had been building between us. Why did I take this chance? Why didn't I realize how much I would love seeing him there, surrounded by my family, a part of my world? I wanted to make him feel a part of something over the holiday, but instead I pushed him too far. Too soon.

"Aidan—"

"Listen, I had a really great time with your family. With you." Then he focused his attention on me, and in his eyes I saw all the doubts I'd felt being confirmed. "But I can't do Christmas with your family. Thanksgiving was hard enough. And please don't misunderstand. I wanted to be there. I wanted to see and experience your family. But at the end of the day, we can't invest in each other's lives in that way. We're not a couple."

Anger and sadness hit me all at once. "I know damn well what we are. We're fun and easy, but nothing about this is serious. Any day now, we'll end things and go back to our own lives, nothing missed. Am I right?"

"It's how it has to be."

"But why? Why can't we change the rules?"

He sighed loudly, then started for the kitchen, grabbed a beer out of the fridge, and took a long pull from it, before setting it down roughly on his counter and spinning around to face me. "It always goes this way, you know? Every single time, yet I never learn."

The anger coiling around in my belly sparked into barely contained rage. "Are you...did you just...?" My head shook as I tried to focus my thoughts, but all I could think about was the Aidan I'd been with over the holiday and how very different this Aidan seemed from him. "You're scared. You know something's happening between us and you don't want to face it, so you'd rather shut it down than give it a shot."

"I'm not shutting it down. I want to be with you. I want this—" he motioned between us—"to continue for as long as you're willing to tolerate me. But you've changed the play without discussing it with me. Little by little, we've edged into this—" His frustration bubbled over and he tossed his hands into the air. "Whatever the hell this is. And now you want more. And you deserve it. If anybody on this fucking planet deserves it, it's you. You lost your father and have spent every day since becoming this driven, intelligent, amazing woman who sees what other people miss. You deserve a man who will give you everything. But I'm not that man. I never will be."

I tried to remain quiet for fear that I would say what was really on my mind, but as soon as I released a breath, the words tumbled out. "You are that man. To me, you're him."

He laughed sarcastically, sat down on his coffee table, and ran his hands through his hair, pulling at the ends before peering back up at me. "Trust me when I say I'm not, and no amount of time will change that. You need to ask yourself if you're still okay with this."

A buzzing sound filled my ears, radiating through me until it found my heart, slowly but surely ripping it apart. I thought I was alone before, surrounded by family and friends, but never feeling the warmth soak in like it should. And then Aidan came home with me, and suddenly I felt it. I understood. I wasn't alone, I was just missing a vital piece of the puzzle, and now I had that piece, and I didn't want to give it up. I didn't want to feel cold. I wanted him, all of him.

"I'm not okay with it."

"Then you have your answer."

The words hit me like an arrow to a bull's-eye.

• • •

I woke the next morning to the feel of dried tears on my cheeks, my pillow cradled in my arms, and Lauren asleep beside me.

I'd spent all night trying to figure out if Aidan and I were over or if this was a fight. And if it was only a fight, what did it mean that we were fighting over something that wouldn't change? I wanted to call him and say I was sorry, beg him to forget everything I'd said. But in the same breath, I wanted to call him and scream at him. I wanted him to admit that we were different, see the changes in us as a step forward instead of shutting it down without even a discussion.

Sure that I couldn't figure anything out before a hot shower and two—okay, three—cups of coffee, I turned on our coffeemaker and slipped into the shower, careful to be quiet so Lauren could sleep. But when I stepped out of the shower twenty minutes later, I found someone else sitting on my bed.

My gaze locked on Aidan, dressed in jeans and a navy plaid button-down, his hands threaded together as he stared back at me. "Lauren let me in. I hope that's okay."

I stopped a few feet from him and crossed my arms. "What are you doing here?"

"I didn't sleep last night. Did you? I kept replaying our conversation over and over, and through it all, I couldn't make sense of a thing. I don't know what I'm fighting here."

A part of me wanted to go to him, to slip into his arms and say we could work things out, somehow, someway, but nothing had changed from last night. I still wanted more than he was willing to give. "You don't have to fight anything. Just ask yourself what you want. It's an easy question."

"It's anything but easy. What I want isn't in line with what I should want. What I feel isn't in line with what I've always thought of myself or my life or my future. I can't make it all fit in my head anymore, and the harder I try the more it scares the shit out of me."

I drew a breath and exhaled slowly. Why couldn't he see that this was easy? I wasn't asking for a marriage proposal. I just wanted to know there was room for possibility, that our future wasn't already set.

"This doesn't have to be so hard," I whispered as I took

a step closer to him, the distance too great for what I had to say next. "What do you want, Aidan? Just tell me what you want. Because I think it's pretty clear what I want, and as tough as it is for me to admit it, the decision isn't mine. It's yours."

"But you see, you've already made the decision. That's the problem. No conversation. No prelude. One minute we agree to *this* and the next you insist on *that*. First with Thanksgiving, then the conversation after and talk of Christmas. All in a few days' time."

I shook my head, frustration sparking again. "I invited you home because I know what it's like to feel alone, and I wanted to show you the kind of home and family you deserve. I didn't mean for it to become...for it to be..."

At that his gaze dropped. "I know. Which was why I should have said no, but I..."

"Couldn't? That should tell you something."

He stared at me, the gold and amber tones in his eyes shining brightly back at me. "I don't know how to do this."

"I know."

"But I don't want it to end."

"Then what do we do?"

Aidan stood and started for me, taking my hands and running his thumbs slowly back and forth over my palms. "I talked to my father's assistant again. He's not doing so well. She asked me to come see him."

"I think you should go see him."

His gaze lifted. "What if you went with me?"

I jerked back. "What? You said we shouldn't invest in each other's lives. You said—"

"I know what I said. But I'm asking you to go anyway. I

need you there. Please…go with me."

I watched his expression change from worry to sadness and knew that I couldn't deny him this. Who knew if his father would survive another attack? Aidan needed to be there, to say whatever he needed to say to him, and if my being there ensured he wouldn't live the rest of his life in guilt, then so be it.

"When do we leave?"

Chapter Twenty-Two

The drive to visit Aidan's father proved to be full of tense silence. I tried to start a conversation, then another. Tried to find music that would soften the mood. But the lines creasing Aidan's forehead never relaxed.

We pulled down a long driveway to a mansion overlooking the canal in Quogue. "This is his house?" I asked, unable to look away from the ginormous house before me. Worn wood and stone covered the two-story exterior, set off by vibrant white trim around large windows that were sure to bring in fantastic lighting.

Aidan followed my gaze up to the house, his hands still on the steering wheel. "One of his houses."

A part of me wanted to ask how many houses he had if this was merely one of them, but then I took in Aidan's pained expression and instead asked, "How long's it been?"

"What?"

"Since you saw him. How long since you saw your

father?"

He sighed. "Four years. We've attended some of the same advertising events, but I've always managed to escape without speaking to him directly."

"Does he know you're coming?"

"Yes. He doesn't appreciate surprises and prefers to stick to a strict schedule. When I was a kid, we had breakfast at seven, lunch at noon, and dinner at six thirty every day. Like clockwork. And if something happened to cause a delay, Mom would hear about it for a week."

I stared down at the clock on the dash. "It's one ten. Are we late?"

His mouth curved into a small smile. "Yes. I wanted to prove a point." He drew a long breath, then peered back over at me. "Are you ready?"

"Whenever you are."

Running his hands down his slacks once, he then pushed from the car and walked around to my side, opening the door for me and helping me out. The front door opened even before we made it past the second step to the flagstone porch.

A petite woman in her early forties greeted us. Her black hair was swept back into a low ponytail, and she was dressed in a narrow pencil skirt and white blouse. She looked as though she'd either just returned from the office or was heading there now.

"It's nice to see you again, Aidan," the woman said, reaching out a hand.

Aidan took it and kissed her cheek. "Whitney, this is Cameron, a friend of mine. Cameron, Whitney is my father's personal assistant."

I nodded a hello to her. "It's nice to meet you." But as I

studied her, I wondered why a personal assistant would be required to stay at her employer's vacation home. It reeked of inappropriate behavior, but I knew better than to ask Aidan about it later.

"He's sitting out on the patio. This way."

I stepped in ahead of Aidan and tried not to gawk at the beauty that was this house. The two-story foyer boasted a vintage-looking chandelier, the wall to our right a large painting of a single sailboat out in an expansive ocean. The painting was decidedly sad, and it made me wonder if there was more to Stuart Graham than appearances and history might suggest. Of course, it could have been a decorator's choice and have little to do with the house's owner.

The foyer led to a large living room with floor-to-ceiling windows, a giant wide-screen hung over a stone fireplace, and white bookshelves rose on either side of the fireplace, both filled with books that appeared much older than the house itself. An ornate rug tied the room together, and two white leather couches sat around the rug in an L-shape. Beyond the furniture and books, there were three wall hangings on the opposite wall from the fireplace, but no photos of people, family, or friends. No photos of Aidan. I wondered if Aidan noticed this as well or if he even cared.

Whitney led us past the kitchen, all stainless steel and granite and as large as half my apartment. Maybe all of it. Lemon and sage and other seasonings I didn't recognize hit my nose, and my stomach rumbled despite my effort to push aside my hunger.

"We'll eat in a few minutes. Is that okay?"

Embarrassed, I nodded. "Of course."

She opened a set of French doors to a flagstone patio

that matched the porch, and immediately her face lit with a smile that was far too unnatural to go unnoticed. Still, my gaze followed hers to the man sitting in a white wicker chair, his eyes focused on the canal.

"You're late," he said.

Whitney started to reply for us when Aidan waved her off. "We're okay."

She didn't look convinced, but she retreated into the house, closing the doors quietly behind her.

"This is Cameron Lawson. Cameron, Stuart Graham."

At that his father's gray eyes lifted to mine. His hair had long since turned white, and though his skin held the remnants of a tan, today his face was as pale as his hair. "Lawson? Any relation to Jeremy Lawson?"

"No, sir. And it's a pleasure to meet you."

He nodded, then threaded his hands together over his stomach and continued his stare over the water. Aidan seemed to understand that response better than me and motioned for us to sit in the matching wicker love seat beside his father. A glass table, trimmed in wicker to match the rest of the set, sat in front of us, and within a minute, Whitney returned with a tray of tea and water.

"It's sweet," she said to me, pointing at the tea. "Aidan mentioned you were in Alabama before, so I thought—" Stuart cleared his throat and Whitney froze, then backed away, an apologetic expression on her face before she disappeared back into the house.

"What, she can't even speak in your presence? She's your PA, for Christ's sake."

Stuart cut his eyes over to Aidan. "If you came here to argue, you can leave."

Aidan released a slow, patient breath. "I came here to check on you. To make sure you're okay."

"I don't need you checking up on me. I'm fine."

Aidan huffed loudly, and I placed a hand on his leg, hoping to settle him. We'd just arrived, and already they were arguing. "I'm the only family you've got, and you suffered a nearly fatal heart attack. Your doctor said it could happen again."

"I see. So you came to talk about your inheritance."

"What? You think I came here for your money? You think I *need* your money?"

"You sound like your mother. Stubborn to the bone. Everyone needs money."

Aidan's jaw locked. "You don't get to talk about her. Do you understand? You are never to talk about her. She loved you, did everything for you, and you left without a backward glance."

Stuart's gaze held on Aidan. "She could never do anything for herself. Like most women. Needy. Insecure. It was exhausting." His eyes drifted to me before returning to Aidan. "I would have expected you to learn this by now. After all, we're exactly the same. Isn't that what the article in *Businessweek* said? 'Like father, like son.'"

Aidan swallowed hard, his hands clenched tightly around his knees, like he needed something to grasp to keep from losing it. "Look, it's been a long time since we talked. I came here because I didn't want the last time I saw you to be us pretending we were strangers at an expo."

"Aren't we strangers? I can't remember the last time you were here, the last time we spoke without yelling."

"And whose fault is that?" Aidan spit out. "But I'm

trying here."

Stuart turned to his son for the first time. "No, what you're trying to do is protect your conscience. Well, consider it cleared. And if you came here for some last-ditch moment with me, some hint at fatherly advice, then here it is: I've got more money than I can spend, and yet I sit here dying with a weak heart. How is that for irony? You go ahead. Conquer the advertising world, and at the end of the day, at the end of your life, you'll be just like me. Married to some spineless woman, with a half version of yourself for a son, and a successful empire that at the end of the day all amounted to nothing."

Aidan stood slowly, like he was seeing his father clearly for the first time. "You know, I always had hope that you would change. That you'd see the error of your ways and become the kind of man I could respect. But no, you are and will always be a self-centered bastard. I came here to try to do the right thing, but I can see that's not possible with you."

Whitney had just come out with our lunch, but Aidan was done. He took my hand, beckoning me to follow him, then stopped beside her. "I'm sorry. I can't stay. Let me know if you need anything. But don't ask me to come here again." Then he closed the door behind us, me fighting to keep pace as we left the house and slipped back into the car.

"Aidan," I said. "We came all this way. Shouldn't you—"

"Did you hear what he just said?"

"Yes, but he's your father."

"So what?" He tossed his hands in the air. "So fucking what? He has never once acted like a fucking father." He focused out the car window, his chest heaving as he tried to rein in his anger. "I can't believe I let Whitney talk me into coming here. This was a mistake. And he's right. We're the exact same, him and me. Which is why I never should have—" He stopped suddenly and swallowed hard before putting the car in drive.

My insides buzzed with dread. "Never should have what?"

His broken gaze turned on me. "I'm not capable of being anything more than that man you saw in there. I've wanted success more than anything, just like him. I crave it. And I refuse to drag you down that path."

"You didn't drag me anywhere. I want to be here."

"I know. But maybe this isn't healthy anymore. Maybe we should…"

"What?"

Aidan stared back out the windshield. "I'm leaving for London tomorrow for three days."

"You're leaving? Why didn't you tell me?"

He shook his head. "I wasn't sure I could leave. But now I think maybe it's good timing."

"Good timing? Are you saying you want to take a break?" My heart hurt with each word, but as I watched Aidan struggle through this tiny visit with his father, I wondered if this was too much for him. For me. I wanted to focus on my career, just like him, and suddenly, all my thoughts were revolving around this man, hoping beyond hope that he would see us clearly. That he'd want to fight for us.

"No. But I want you to think about this and if it's really what you want."

Crossing my arms, I settled back into my seat without responding, afraid to look at him for fear I would show just how much this hurt me.

How could two days have changed so much?

Chapter Twenty-Three

"You are not going to believe what I just heard," Alexa said as she slipped into my cubicle. Monday came too quickly, and even though I knew I needed to put on a happy "my life rocks" face, I couldn't ignore how sad I felt. Aidan left for London with a quick text that he would miss me, but I refused to allow the words to settle in my heart like they should. I didn't want to focus on what he felt for me, and I for him, when it could all be over the moment he returned.

I spun around in my chair and peered behind her to make sure no one was walking by. "What did you hear?"

She lowered her voice and leaned in. "They want Aidan to take over the London office."

The pen I'd been twirling in my hand dropped from my grasp, and I scrambled to pick it up from the ground—along with my jaw. "The London office? I thought he was just going for three days?" She had to be mistaken. Aidan would have told me. Right?

Her eyebrows threaded together. "How did you know he'd be gone for three days? No one seemed to know where he was this morning other than Dorothy and Gayle."

Shit. "Oh, um, he mentioned it in our last meeting," I said, hoping my voice sounded even.

Alexa shrugged. "Well, I'm betting he's over there to talk about the move. I bet he's already accepted it. And who could blame him? I can only imagine how much money they're offering."

"There are more important things than money."

She laughed. "Yeah, like what? At least for him? He's single. There's nothing keeping him here. He'd be crazy to turn it down."

I opened my mouth to argue with her and realized that there was nothing to argue—at least not for work Cameron. Work Cameron shouldn't care what Aidan did. She should be as interested in the gossip as Alexa. But in the moment, all I wanted to do was call him and ask if it was true, if this was the real reason for our arguments the last two days. Was he trying to find an easy out so he could go to London without any guilt? And who could blame him for wanting the job? He'd control that office, make more money, and further prove to his father that he could be successful without the Graham name.

"Hey…are you all right? You look pale," Alexa said.

I swallowed hard. "Yeah. Absolutely. I was just thinking about a project creative is working on this morning for me. I need to go check on it. Want to do lunch?"

"For sure. See you in a few," she said as she rushed off.

My phone buzzed from beside my computer, and I peered down to find a new text from Aidan. *Meetings all day, but I want to talk. Call you tonight?*

Right, meetings to discuss you moving there, I wanted to text back, but I didn't want to ask him about it over text or on the phone. For now, I had to hold this in until we could talk about it in person. The sad thing was that he'd been gone all of a day, and I already missed him terribly. Three days was going to feel like an eternity, but then, I'd have to prepare myself for the hard fact that our relationship was hitting its expiration date. Stupidly, I convinced myself that Aidan's fears about us were his way of trying to protect me. But now I learned that Aidan was moving to London. Would he wait to break it off, or give me the news over the phone tonight?

The thought made my heart clench tight, bracing itself for the pain to come. I read the text again, unsure of how to respond without giving away my thoughts. This wasn't supposed to happen. This was supposed to be fun and easy—casual. When did my heart get involved?

And that was the real issue. My heart had always been involved, because I wasn't a casual kind of girl. I wanted what my parents had, what my mom had with Eric. I wanted love and commitment and willingness to push through the hard stuff. The problem was, I also wanted Aidan, and he didn't want those things. So what did that mean for us?

I pressed the phone to my forehead, frustrated that I had to wait to talk to him. I wanted to hash this out now. But now wasn't an option, so I simply typed back, *Tonight*, and clicked send.

Never had one word held so much dread.

• • •

Lauren and Alexa were already seated at the restaurant when I arrived for lunch. With Aidan out of the office and Gayle leaving early for the day, I felt more at ease taking a proper, hour-long lunch without feeling guilty.

I sat down and tried to listen in to their conversation.

"You should totally apply," Lauren said before taking a drink of her water.

"I can't. There are no open positions."

A waitress came by to take my drink order, and as soon as she walked away I asked, "What position? Where?"

Alexa sank back into her chair. "It's stupid. But I really want to move up at Sanderson-Lowe. I want to be an account manager, but there are no open positions right now."

"Oh. Well, what about other positions? I saw something open up in creative a few weeks ago."

She shook her head. "I know nothing about design, but I think I'm good with clients. I've been trying to pay attention to the latest campaigns, to learn. Do you think you could put in a good word for me with Gayle? Oh! Or better yet, Aidan? He seems to really like you."

At that Lauren began to choke on her drink, sputtering. I shot her a look that said *zip it or else*, and then focused back on Alexa. "Definitely. I'm sure they'd consider you if a position opened up."

"I hope so," she said. "I don't want to be an administrative assistant forever. I know I can do more. I just need to focus on finding a way."

My eyebrows drew together. "What do you mean 'a way'?"

She shrugged. "Well, Peyton, that new AM under Brody, is always late. I bet Brody would have an issue with it if a little birdie told him." She grinned wickedly, and I shook my head.

"You can't out her like that. It wouldn't be right."

Lauren and I both stared at Alexa, waiting for her to agree, but she simply shrugged again, her look distant, and I wondered if she was planning that very thing in hopes of scoring Peyton's job. The thought sent a chill over me as I realized how little I knew of Alexa or what she was capable of. I'd have to be much, much more careful.

Chapter Twenty-Four

That night I slipped into my apartment and set down my keys and purse, exhausted from the stress of the day—and none of it technically had anything to do with work. I contemplated calling Aidan a thousand times, texting him, anything to relieve the urge in me to know. But each time, I set my phone back down, my eyes returning to the word "tonight," and the sinking feeling would start all over again.

The apartment was empty, Lauren out on another date with Patrick, and in the quiet I found myself spiraling faster into my misery. When did this happen to me? When did my happiness become linked to a guy? Even with Blaine, I kept myself focused, centered. But this was different. Aidan was different. I felt so unbelievably happy around him, so at peace. I didn't want to give that up. At first, I thought my comfort was because he understood my goals—his being so similar—but it was never about the job. It was him. The easy way he looked at me, the way he willingly opened up about his life, the way he listened to me talk about my dad without the smallest hint of pity on his face. I didn't want to lose that.

I didn't want to lose him.

Tears clouded my vision, and I started for my bathroom for a tissue just as my phone vibrated against the counter. It was just after seven, after midnight in London. He'd stayed awake for me.

Grabbing my phone, I curled up on the couch, hitting answer even before I looked at the screen. "Hey…"

"Hey, yourself," he said, his voice low, tired.

"Busy day?" I asked. "You sound exhausted."

"Just a day of difficult decisions. Always the toughest to get through. Listen, I wanted to talk about—"

"I know."

He hesitated on the other end, the sounds of him breathing making it hard for me to keep from blurting out every thought I had about London and him and us. But again, it wasn't my conversation.

"Cameron…"

"It's okay."

"It is?"

My heart plummeted into my stomach. He sounded only marginally disappointed, nothing more. My pride wouldn't allow me to tell him how much I wanted him to stay if he wasn't thinking the same thing. If he wasn't just as desperate to be with me. Here I'd stupidly thought he'd take a chance on me, drop the no-dating thing for me, but now I saw I'd been as foolish as all the women before me.

"I get that it's a great opportunity. You'd be crazy to turn it down. And besides, we were just having fun, right?" My voice shook with emotion, and I wondered if he could hear it, if he knew how much this was breaking me.

"I'm not sure—"

"Really. I'm fine with it." Lies. All lies.

"What exactly are you talking about?"

I sat up and crossed my legs. What was his game? He knew exactly what I was talking about. Did he want to hear me say it? "London," I spit out.

"Right… And I get why you might be disappointed, but why are you so angry?"

Disappointed? The nerve. Poor little Cameron, disappointed that *the* Aidan Truitt is dumping her. "Look, I'm really tired. I'll talk to you—"

"I swear to God if you hang up this phone, I will fly home and come knock on your door. I don't avoid things, Cameron. And I don't appreciate being left in the dark. What is—"

"You're moving to London."

"I'm what?"

"Alexa told me at the office today. They offered you an amazing job and an amazing salary and now you're moving. And I get it. I do. I just…" I trailed off, unable to say what I was truly thinking, feeling.

He started to laugh, and for the first time ever, I contemplated dipping into Dad's money just so I could buy a private flight over to his hotel so I could kick his ass.

"It's not funny."

"No, you're right. You believing gossip at the office instead of coming to me directly *isn't* funny."

I swallowed hard. "I was waiting for you to tell me, but you weren't admitting it."

"That's because there's nothing to admit. I called to tell you that I'd be here two more days, arriving back to New

York on Friday. I know things have been off between us, so I didn't want you to think I was staying to avoid you. The opposite, actually. I'm dying to get back home."

I jerked upright, my heart beginning to dance and cheer in excitement. "It's not true?"

"No. They've offered. But they've been offering for a year now. My life is in New York."

Relief swarmed through me, relaxing the tension in my shoulders. "I would kiss you right now if I could."

"I would do a lot more than kiss you. I miss you."

"But what about the rules, the complications?"

"I don't know. I just know that I'm sitting here alone in my hotel room, and all I want in the world is for you to be here, too."

My bottom lip trembled, and I swallowed hard to try to push away my emotions so I could speak. "So what should we do now?"

"No clue. You?"

"No clue," I whispered.

Chapter Twenty-Five

My legs jumped as my fingers tapped against the bar in time to the music. Lauren, Alexa, and Grace insisted we go out. After all, it was a Friday and we were young twentysome-things, each of us single, though Lauren had dated Patrick pretty exclusively for the past few weeks.

I tapped my nails harder against the wood of the bar, and Lauren reached for my hand, stopping me. She glanced around to make sure we were alone—the other girls were already on the dance floor. "When does he arrive?"

"What? Who?"

She cocked her head. "You know who. You're doing that nervous tap thing you do, where your mind is a million miles away, and you can't sit still. When does he get in?"

I shrugged. "His flight landed a half hour ago."

"Then why are you here?"

"I'm waiting on him to call me."

She eyed the dance floor. "You don't have to wait on

him."

"But, what if—?"

"Cameron, he cares about you. I know it's complicated, but he does care about you. You don't have to wait on him to call. This isn't all on him. You have to tell him what you want, and if you care about him, too, you have to be willing to work things out."

"He doesn't want to commit."

"Yeah, but he's not with anyone else, either."

I stared at Lauren, who cocked her head in that see-I-know-all way. But she was right. He wasn't seeing anyone else. And despite everything, I didn't want to be with just anyone. I wanted Aidan. And though he wasn't ready for the whole forever thing, maybe if I pointed out to him that we were already exclusive, that it wasn't scary, and that I wasn't brokenhearted, then he would see that he could have a healthy relationship. It might require patience, but Aidan was capable of commitment. I knew it in my heart, and if Dad had taught me anything, it was that I needed to trust my heart.

I smiled as I focused on Lauren. "I'm going to go see him."

She smiled back. "I'd already be gone."

• • •

I called Aidan from outside his apartment, my nerves still coiled tight from the decisions I'd made. It never occurred to me before that I needed to help Aidan through this. If I cared about him, then I had to care about him enough to wait. We may not be in a strict, committed relationship, but we were something. I could feel it, and I wasn't ready to let go.

He answered on the first ring. "I was hoping you would come," he said, his voice low as he buzzed me in, and then I was rushing into his building and onto the elevator, my foot tapping the entire way. It wasn't until the elevator doors opened that I realized what I'd done. I'd just ridden on an elevator, without freaking out, without singing, without even a second thought. The realization that my desperation to see him had overcome my fear was enough to send me running down the hall.

Aidan pulled me into his arms the moment I crossed the threshold into his apartment. It had been five days with him in London, me here, and in that time, one thing became abundantly clear: I didn't want this to end. I was ready to fight for what I wanted.

I rose onto my toes and kissed him with urgency, unable to stop myself, and then he lifted me into his arms and began walking toward his bedroom, his thoughts in line with mine. He set me down on the edge of the king-size bed and peered down and dear God, that simple look, so full of want, was my undoing.

"I care about you, and I know you care for me, too. We don't have to follow any rules at all. We can take our time and let this, whatever it is, become whatever we want it to become. We don't have to know right now. And maybe it ends anyway, but how can we let it end without trying?"

Aidan tilted my chin up and ran his thumb slowly over my bottom lip, his gaze following his thumb before locking on my eyes. "We can't."

Warmth spread through me. Forget talking. Forget

kissing. I wanted to feel connected to him in every way, body and mind. I wanted to forget about what Alexa had said, forget about my job, forget about how it felt like I was walking in the middle of the street, bound to get hit any moment. For that second, I just wanted Aidan. And he wasn't nearly close enough.

I stood up and ran my fingers down his tie. It was the red one I loved, and I smiled at my memory of the first time I'd seen it—the things I'd pictured him doing with it.

"I love this tie," I said, my voice sultry.

Aidan's eyes grew dark, drinking me in. "Oh yeah?" He shook out of his suit jacket and loosened the tie, then he leaned down and pressed his lips to my neck and whispered, "I'd rather see you wearing it…and nothing else."

Desire raged through me, settling low in my core. "I think I can arrange that."

I stepped away from him and took my time pulling off my sweater and slinking out of my leggings, careful to keep my eyes on him the entire time. His gaze swept over me as I unfastened my bra and let it fall to the floor, so I was before him in only a thong, him still fully dressed in business attire. I walked slowly toward him and reached for the tie, but he shook his head.

"Lie down."

The fire simmering low in my belly burst into wild flames at the command in his voice. I lay back on his bed, enjoying the feel of his eyes on me. I expected him to undress and join me, but instead he sat beside me and ran a hand over my face, down my breasts, and then finally cupping my heat, allowing his fingers to glide over me again and again until I was ready to explode.

"Lift your arms and cross them at the wrist."

I hesitated for a moment, unsure where this was going, but I was far too turned on to ask questions. I did as he asked, and then he leaned over me and began threading the tie around my wrists, binding them above my head. *Dear God...*

Aidan walked to the end of his bed and peered down at me. "So beautiful. I can't get enough of you. No amount of time with you will ever be enough." Then he crawled up the bed, still fully clothed, and I could see that he intended to take his time. The feel of his smooth duvet below my nearly naked body and Aidan over me was enough to make me writhe with each touch, but he didn't give in. Instead, he trailed his hands slowly over me, careful to show attention to every inch of my skin. His tongue swept up my left calf, inside my thigh. His fingers delicately trailed down my abdomen, over the edges of my thong. I started to drop my arms down and he pulled away, letting me know that to get what I wanted, what I craved, I had to follow his rules.

My arms dropped back down above my head and I arched my back, eager to feel his touch again. He didn't disappoint. His mouth dipped down, taking one nipple, then the other, the kisses slow, careful—agonizing.

"Your skin is so soft," he said, caressing my breast, then tracing the dip of my waist with his tongue, then his hand slipped inside my thong, and every sensible thought in my mind was replaced with *yes, yes, yes.* His fingers moved over my mound, across my slick folds, and then he pulled his hand away quickly, and I started to beg him to continue when he slowly slid my thong off, kissing my hip, then thigh, then foot, before tossing it aside, exposing me fully and driving me to a place of passion I'd never been before.

"Aidan…"

And then his clothes were off and he was reaching for his nightstand for protection and then with one rough thrust he was inside me, filling me completely. He grabbed my bound hands with one hand, anchoring me down with his strength and sending my insides spiraling out of control. Our bodies moved together as he thrust still deeper and deeper, knowing just where I needed him, and I screamed out, unable to remain quiet. My body buzzed with desire, desperate for a release, and then Aidan's mouth clamped down over mine, the kiss full of all the emotions I longed to say, and I exploded, fireworks everywhere, body gone, mind gone, everything in me lost to this man above me.

Aidan untied my wrists and relaxed beside me, pulling me close, and I felt my bottom lip quiver for reasons I couldn't understand, tears threatening to fall. An overwhelming sensation moved over me, my emotions and body pushed to their max. I drew a shaky breath, and he rose up to look at me. "Are you okay? Did I hurt you?"

I shook my head, not trusting myself to speak just yet.

His expression twisted as he scanned my face for answers. "Cameron, what is it?"

I stared back at him, at the care in his eyes, and the words were right there, on the tip of my tongue, ready to put myself out there. Ready to take a chance on this, on Aidan. "I…" But then I thought of how horrible I'd felt when I thought he was leaving me, and how much worse that would have been if he'd known the truth. If he'd known that I loved him. "Did you mean what you said before? That you're willing to try?" I finally asked, taking a small step. A chance. Not the word "love," but a chance all the same. A declaration toward what I wanted out of this relationship and out of my life. It was okay for me to want a serious relationship, and it was okay for me to want that with Aidan.

He kissed my lips sweetly and settled down beside me, cradling me to him. "I don't know how to do this."

I'd heard him say that before, but we were adults. We learned things we didn't understand. We didn't simply shut down. "I know, but we can figure it out together."

"What if we can't? What if we start this and slowly but surely I turn into my father. What then? How could I allow that to happen to you?"

"It's no different than work, Aidan. If you were like him, you would have fallen into your rightful place at GG. You chose Sanderson-Lowe. You can choose this. Us. And I'm not saying it will be easy, but the choice is yours. Not his. Yours." I paused, letting that digest before I hit him with the next thing on my mind. Fear worked through my chest as the words held on to my tongue. It was time to take the next step, and either he followed, or I said good-bye. As much as it hurt to think about, I knew I couldn't continue like this.

"Come home with me for Christmas."

"Cameron—"

I pressed my fingertips to his lips. "Let me finish. If you still feel this is a bad idea, then we go our separate ways. But you shouldn't be alone over the holiday, and you know, in your heart, you want to go with me. Trust yourself. Not the person you think you'll become, but the person you are right here, today."

His head tilted to the side as he considered it, his eyes unfocused, deep in thought and no doubt worry. "What if I hurt you?" he whispered.

"I won't let you. I'll walk away."

"How many days will we be there?"

I swallowed, forcing my voice to remain even, devoid of the hope swirling through my belly. "One week."

"One week with you? I won't be able to walk away."

I leaned down and pressed my lips to his. "I hate when you say things like that."

And then taking comfort in our small step, I slumped down beside him, snuggling into the crook of his neck, and fell fast asleep.

Chapter Twenty-Six

The winter air proved colder for a Christmas in Birmingham than expected, and I was thankful as Aidan and I stepped outside at the airport that I'd packed lots of warm clothes. Instantly, the familiar smells of home came wafting back to me. Smells of pine trees and clean, crisp air. I wondered if Aidan felt the change, too. We were just here, yet going back to the crowded city made these things all the more noticeable.

The stress of our return to New York was followed by an almost animallike desire to be together. It was like we sensed our relationship rising to that pivotal point where a decision had to be made—move forward or say good-bye. And neither of us was ready to go.

I spotted Eric's Tahoe in the pickup lane a few cars back and motioned to Aidan. "There they are."

Eric stepped out as we approached to help with our bags. I hugged him, and then he shook Aidan's hand. "Nice to have you back."

"Nice to be back."

We slipped into the Tahoe, and I started to ask where Mom was just as Eric launched into all things football. They talked football for the rest of the drive, and by the time we reached our house, Aidan was grinning and Eric was talking animatedly with his hands. I settled into my seat as I watched them, thinking I could get used to this.

Mom met us on the front steps, and Aidan reached for her hand, but she swept him into a tight hug. "Merry Christmas!"

Aidan looked taken aback, but then he relaxed into the hug and swallowed hard. "Merry Christmas, Lorelei."

She turned her attention on me, hugging me close. "I missed you."

"It's only been a few weeks."

"Too many weeks. Well, come on in. I have dinner on the stove and hot cider made for after."

My mouth dropped as we stepped inside. Mom had always been an amazing decorator, but Christmas brought out something deeper in her style. The house smelled of cinnamon and nutmeg. The foyer table displayed one of four of her Christmas villages, the lights and sounds twinkling and dinging as we passed. The staircase had been dusted with its own Christmas decor—the banisters were draped with garland and red berries and lights. The long running rug that led from the front door to the great room had been replaced with one with a motif of Santa giving out presents to kids. Neil Diamond's "Happy Christmas (War is Over)" played in the background, joined in by the occasional crackle of the fire in the great room. I shook my head as I faced Mom. "You outdid yourself this year. It's amazing."

She shrugged me off, never one to properly accept a compliment, but the smile on her face proved her pleasure at my reaction. "Well, the family'll be here on Christmas Eve and then again Christmas Day for lunch, and you know they come expecting."

I turned back to Aidan, prepared to point him to the dining room table, when the look on his face stopped me short. He focused on every carefully decorated detail. The nutcrackers on the mantel. The snowman afghan on the back of the couch. And then his eyes landed on the massive Christmas tree, no less than twelve feet tall, in the far corner of the great room. I thought of all the things he missed growing up and gripped his hand, showing I was there if he needed me. But then he smiled. Maybe instead of making him sad, this was showing him what a real family looked like—what we could look like someday.

"Let's eat."

After family updates and lots of laughter, we finished dinner and enjoyed cider in front of the fire, before Mom and Eric said they were going to bed.

"Stay up as long as you like. You won't disturb us," Mom said as she closed the door behind her.

Aidan and I went on upstairs, and as soon as we heard their door close downstairs, he took a step toward me and pressed his lips to mine. "I've been waiting to do that all night," he said.

"Oh really? What else have you been waiting to do?"

"This," he said, kissing my neck. "And this." His hands ran down my back, and he pulled me close. "I like your family. A lot."

I nodded against his shoulder, feeling overwhelmed

with emotion. "Me, too."

Aidan looked at me. "What is it?"

"Nothing." I shook my head. "I'm just very happy."

"Me, too."

We held each other for a long moment before Aidan pulled back, his eyes on the adjoining door. "Meet back in here in a few?"

"Dirty."

"I hope so."

With a laugh, I went for the main door, a mischievous smile on my face. "I'm going to get ready for bed. Good night."

Closing the door, I felt like a sixteen-year-old again, desperate to keep my parents from hearing me sneak out of the house to meet a boy. Only this time the boy wasn't waiting at some party for me. He was next door, and there was nothing boyish about him. Aidan was all man, full of want and desire. Heat coursed through me at the thought. I ached to have him near me, touching me, kissing me.

Once inside, I slipped out of my clothes and draped them across the vanity chair. I thought of putting on a nightgown, but stopped at my reflection in the mirror, at my red lace bra and matching red thong. I pulled my hair out of my ponytail and let it flow down over my shoulders, then walked through our adjoining bathroom and knocked quietly on his door so as not to alert the parents below.

Aidan opened the door and stepped back, his eyes drinking me in, warming my body.

"Merry Christmas," I said.

"I'll say."

My nipples hardened as he focused on my breasts, and

I edged closer to him, ready to feel him over me. He hadn't undressed at all, and was still wearing his dress slacks and pressed collared shirt. I slowly undid each button until his shirt fell off him, then ran my hands down the front of his pants, stopping at the evidence of his need. I unbuckled his belt and dropped his pants, then walked him back to the bed. He lifted me up so I straddled his waist.

"You are so unbelievably beautiful," he said, and then there was no more talking. He lips crushed against mine, and he laid me back against the bed, our bodies connecting. I longed to tell him that I loved him, but the words caught in my throat. Admitting out loud how much I cared made it real. And it made the possibility of him pulling back real. He might not be ready to hear those words, and then what? For now, I tugged him back to me, allowing my body to show him what I was too afraid to say. Saving the words for a safer time.

Chapter Twenty-Seven

Mom and I spent most of the morning prepping for Christmas Eve dinner. When I was younger, we would go to my grandmother's house on Christmas Eve and take turns opening presents around her tree. Once she passed away, my mom took over the family meal, and so for years now, our house has become home to more and more people on Christmas Eve, some family, others friends who had no family of their own to celebrate with. Much like Aidan. All in all, we had four eight-person tables decorated throughout the house.

Mom slipped outside to clip more greenery, and Aidan came up behind me, wrapping his arms tightly around me. "This is a good look on you," he said, tapping my apron.

"You think so?" I turned in his arms and pressed a quick kiss to his lips, planning to separate before Mom returned, when she spoke from the back door.

"I see one couple that'll make use of my mistletoe. Now, Aidan, Eric is going into town to pick up a few last-minute things. Do you think you could help him?"

"Of course." He kissed my temple before disappearing out the front door in search of Eric.

Mom resumed her place beside me chopping vegetables, a silent smile on her face.

"What?" I asked, unable to stay quiet any longer.

She set down her knife and turned to me. "I have watched you for years now, Cammie. I've watched boys come and go. Friends come and go. I've seen you at your highest highs, like when you were accepted at NYU. And your lowest lows, like when your father died." She cleared her throat. "Through all of that, I've waited to see you happy again. Truly happy. And not once have I felt you were. Not even with Blaine. Lord knows, we've tried, but nothing has sparked a smile like the one you wear whenever Aidan's around. I'm thankful for him. I'm thankful to see you happy again."

"Mom."

"Look, Cameron. I know you and I haven't always seen eye to eye. Your father's death…" She trailed off, her eyes brimming with tears. I had never once seen my mother cry over Dad's death, beyond at the funeral itself. "I have tried so hard to help you get over it, when maybe the right thing was to help you through it. I guess I've always been jealous of your dad."

"Why?"

She cleared her throat again and dabbed the corners of her eyes with a paper towel. "Because you love him so purely. As selfish as it sounds, I wanted a bit of that love."

Guilt punctured my heart like a knife. "Mom…I…I'm sorry. I didn't mean to make you feel like I didn't love you. Of course I love you." I pulled her into a hug. "I just…I don't know, but I'm sorry."

Mom waved me off and smiled. "Under the rug. Let's forget about it. It's Christmas."

I smiled back. "It's Christmas."

. . .

Guests began arriving at five that night, and before long, the house was full of people of all ages. Children ran around the rooms, chasing each other. Adults enjoyed drinks and mingled. All while Mom swept from room to room, checking that glasses were full and people were happy.

I introduced Aidan to everyone who hadn't already met him, and beyond a painful conversation with Uncle Buck about all the reasons why the Democrats were ruining America, they had all been nice.

Then my cousins arrived, and though they had been good on Thanksgiving, their claws were ready to strike today. Lexie and Anna Beth took no time coming over to us, their eyes roaming over Aidan in ways that would make both their husbands angry.

"So, Aidan," Anna Beth drawled. "Tell us how you met our sweet Cammie."

Sweet Cammie? Clearly she was after an Oscar with this performance. Aidan grinned over at me, sensing my unease. I wanted to disappear with him upstairs, to relieve some of my stress. But the house was full of people, and I was too much my mother's daughter to show such horrible manners, despite the hating cousins drooling over Aidan. And that was when I realized I hadn't been paying attention to the conversation, and now our audience had grown to include my aunts.

"Sorry, what did you say?" Aunt Trudy asked, her face pinched. "You're Cammie's *boss*?"

Crap. We hadn't discussed how to handle this second visit, and now… "No, he's not my boss. He's…" I trailed off, a cold sweat breaking out on my back. Their eyes were all on me, waiting.

I opened my mouth, though I had no idea what I wanted to say, when Mom called out from the kitchen doorway, her hand outstretched, pointing at something above us. Our heads all tilted up, and there, right above Aidan and me, was a bundle of mistletoe. Mom beamed at me. "It's the house rule. You must kiss if you're under mistletoe."

Aidan's gaze fixed on me. "Gladly." And in one swift move, he pulled me to him, kissing me sweetly, not willing to let go, and suddenly the aunts were sighing and the cousins were walking away, and I peered over at Mom in time to catch her winking at me before heading back into the kitchen. She'd looked out for me, saved me.

My chest felt heavy as a surge of emotions worked through me. "I'll be right back," I said to Aidan before heading to the kitchen. Mom was alone, her strict *one cook in the kitchen* rule enforced.

She cocked her head at me. "I'm not letting you try the pecan pie before it's on the table, Cammie. So you can just turn your cute bottom around and go back to that boy of yours."

I came up to her and, before she could say another word, wrapped my arms around her, tears glistening my eyes. "I love you so much."

She set down the wooden spoon she had in her hand and

turned to me. "What in the world is this?" she asked.

"I just…I love you. And I miss you. And I'm sorry that I don't always make you proud. But every success I've ever had is because you were there for me. Even when you didn't like what I did. You supported me. I love you, Mom."

She smiled, her own tears in her eyes, though I knew today of all days she'd never cry. She was a hostess today. "You're wrong." I drew back, and she gripped my hand. "I am so proud of you. Of everything you've done, of the woman you are becoming. I couldn't be more proud."

I hugged her again, getting flour from her apron on my blouse, but I didn't care.

"I love you," she said, then with a soft kiss to my cheek and a little sniffle she added, "Now, get out of my kitchen."

Dinner was served at six, like always, and then we all ate dessert and listened while Eric read *'Twas the Night Before Christmas* to all the children. Aidan pulled me against him as we listened and kissed my neck, and I could get used to him here, in my world. He fit into the crazy, somehow. He fit me.

"I have a surprise for you," he said into my ear. I stiffened instantly. We'd agreed to no presents, and though I knew my parents would have something for him tomorrow, I'd kept to the agreement, fearful that opening gifts might remind him of his mom, and I didn't want to make him sad on Christmas.

"But, we—"

"Shh," Aidan said, pressing a finger to my lips. "This is the best part."

I focused back on Eric as he finished up the story and passed around the small gifts Mom had bought all the kids. They opened them up excitedly, and then the house was empty and we were cleaning up so Mom and Eric could go on to bed.

"You do the family thing well," Aidan said from where he stood drying the china I'd just washed.

I grinned. "You're not so bad at it yourself."

His eyes fixed on me and he walked over, pinning me to the counter, his arms on either side of me. "I like this. Being here with you. In the open."

My gaze dropped. "Yeah, me, too."

He lifted my chin and peered into my eyes. "Tell me what you're thinking. Why do you look sad?"

I hesitated. I'd told him how I felt in a roundabout way, but he hadn't given me anything to go on. Still, Christmas Eve didn't feel like the right time to push it. "It's nothing."

The house had become chilly without the fire in the great room to keep us warm, and I shivered. Aidan ran his hands up and down my arms to try to warm me. "Tell me."

"I don't want this to end," I finally admitted. "And…" I hesitated again, wishing I could hold this in for another day, until we returned back home, until the magic of Christmas was gone and we were back to reality.

"And?"

"I don't want to hide anymore. I don't want to kiss you in abandoned stairwells or hide in closets or be afraid to bring you home to my apartment because Alexa might be there. I want this. I want a family and kids. I want it all."

He stared down at me and ran his hands easily through my hair, a storm of mixed emotions in his eyes, before he finally blinked hard and said, "What if we talked about moving in together? Focused on this version of us, worked to make it more. I can do long-term. With you, I can. But…" He drew a long breath, his arms back at his side, like he needed to separate from me to say his next words. "I can't get married. I can't have kids. Those things aren't in my future."

I fought to swallow as a mix of emotions hit me. There was a time I would have been thrilled with his offer, would have clung to it with the hope that one day it would become more. But I wasn't a girl anymore, who wished on stars and prayed for things to change. Adulthood meant discovering not only who you were, but what you wanted out of your life. I knew what I wanted now. I couldn't go back. "I know this is big for you."

"It is."

I hesitated, but if I didn't get it out now, I never would. "I'm sorry, it's not enough for me. I have to know this is going somewhere. I…" I sucked in a breath, tears pricking my eyes, but I couldn't deny this any longer. "I don't want to be with anyone else. I want you. But…I want a husband more. I want kids. I want to grow old with someone and watch our kids grow up. I want a lifetime."

He took a step back, shutting down. "You know I can't offer you that."

"Why? How do you know you can't?"

"I've been honest from the beginning, and if you're going to keep demanding things from me that I can't give, then it's best we end this now. I don't want to hurt you."

"But you are hurting me. You're not even trying."

"I *am* trying. It's just not enough for you."

"No, you're letting your fear of failure control your life. You decide what kind of man you're going to be. One day at a time, you decide your future. Whether or not you turn into your father is up to you." And then with one long look at him, one last chance for him to ask me to stay, I walked away.

Chapter Twenty-Eight

"Cameron," Gayle said from the doorway to the break room. "We have a new client arriving in fifteen. Do you think you could sit in on the meeting?"

I nodded. "Sure."

She smiled. "Fantastic. See you in there."

It was Monday after Christmas break, and it had taken every ounce of my strength to go into the office. I brought the photo of Dad and me home and set it on my nightstand, needing him with me. His face, the person he'd been and the person he wanted me to be, was the only reason I managed to get out of bed.

It had been three days without a single word from Aidan, and though I'd broken down and sent him a text, he hadn't replied. At this point, I had no idea what we were anymore, if anything at all.

The door to the break room opened, and I peered over to see Alexa rushing in. "Guess what?" she exclaimed.

I shook my head. "What?"

She pulled back, studying my face. "Why do you look so miserable?"

"What? Oh…I was disappointed to leave my family."

She shrugged, and I realized she did that a lot. Like whatever I said wasn't important enough to cause her more thought. It grated on my nerves, but I didn't say anything. "Gayle just told me that she wasn't hiring just yet, but as soon as a position opened up, it would be mine! Me. I can almost see the title behind my name now. And the money! Geez, I could really use the money."

Not to disappoint her, but we lowly account managers didn't make much money. Surely she didn't expect some massive increase, right? By the look on her face, I'd say that was exactly what she expected. Sighing, I went to make my coffee when my phone buzzed with a text. I fumbled to check the call, only to find a new text from Mom.

I shoved my phone back into my pocket, wishing Aidan would respond with something, anything, so I wouldn't feel so lost. "Are they expanding, then?" I asked Alexa, eager to talk about something to get my mind off Aidan. "I think I'm Gayle's only account manager."

"You are. Do you have any skeletons in your closet I can exploit?" She started laughing, and I glared at her. "I'm kidding. Well, I'm off to prove I rock. See you around."

I stared after her, shaking my head. Aidan and I were over now, so I didn't have any skeletons to worry about. Pushing out of the break room, I started down the hall, hopeful that I could make it to my cube without—

My thoughts cut short as my gaze locked on his. We were six feet from each other, no more, but never had I felt further away from him. His mouth opened, and then his gaze found the floor, and I knew without him having to say anything that we had passed into the awkward after zone. I was an idiot to text him and hope we could resolve things. Clearly, for him, we were already done.

"Cameron…"

"See you in the meeting." I walked around him and sat down at my desk, my hands trembling. My phone buzzed again, and I prepared to quickly text Mom back that I'd call her later when my gaze locked on the text.

Aidan: *I'm sorry.*

I wanted to ask him for which part, but I was afraid that if I started the conversation I wouldn't be able to stop without ending up in tears, and I refused to cry here. For now, I had to push this aside, ignore him, go back to the way things were before. But how could I go back?

I couldn't.

Thankfully, the meeting with the new client went well, and the rest of the day breezed by, Aidan in and out of meetings all day, so I barely saw him, saving me from any more painful run-ins. It had gotten late fast, and, exhausted, I started for the elevator, finally comfortable enough to ride it again, when Aidan slipped in after me. "Wait." He leaned into me as the elevator began to drop. "I didn't want you to ride alone."

"I'm fine."

"Are you? Because I'm not. I thought about what you said all weekend. That I decide the man I want to be. And I don't want to be the kind of man who hurts you, who walks away from you. I don't want this to end. Anything is possible if we're willing to fight for it. And I am, Cameron. You asked me to try. Now I'm asking you to do the same. I miss you. I—"

Before he could continue, I rose onto my toes and crushed my lips to his, unsure of anything else, but I couldn't stay away from him another second. I missed him too much to stay away. His smell, his laugh, the feel of his warm body against mine. And before either of us could think better of it, the kiss turned frenzied, his hands in my hair, my body flush against his, all thought and reason gone except for us and this moment.

Which was why I didn't hear the elevator *ping* open. Or the sound of someone clearing her throat from just outside its doors. We flew apart like two teenagers caught by their parents, smiles on our lips, until we caught sight of the person before us, and the smiles quickly turned to horror.

Alexa stood outside the elevator doors, her eyebrows drawn together in a glare, her arms crossed. "Well, I guess this explains why you've been doing so well," she spit out. "It's easy to succeed when you're in bed with the boss."

I sucked in a sharp breath. "No—it's not—we're not—"

"Save it," she said, seething. "I've worked my ass off for a year now, only to be passed over again and again. And you? You come in here, win everyone over, and now I find out you're screwing Aidan, too? I can't even look at you. I'll get my coat tomorrow." She spun around and started for the main doors, me rushing after her.

"Alexa, listen. Stop. Stop!"

But she was already outside, grabbing a cab, and then gone. Finally she had the juice she needed to get someone fired. I just never thought that someone would be me.

• • •

"Stop worrying," Aidan said.

"I'm not worrying."

"Then why won't you look at me?"

I glanced up at him from where I sat on the floor of his apartment, a makeshift plate of Chinese takeout on the coffee table in front of me. The smells, which had always made my stomach rumble in delight, were now nauseating. How could I eat right now?

"How are you eating?" I asked, unable to hide the bite in my tone.

"Easy." Aidan lifted his chopsticks slowly to his mouth, making a show of chewing. "Like this. The question is, why aren't you?"

I jumped to my feet, my frustration bubbling over. "Alexa knows! She knows. And now I'm going to be fired and you're going to be fired and we're going to be unable to get new jobs at agencies because of our non-competes and— Oh my God. You're going to have to go work for your dad, and—"

Aidan was to me now, taking my hands in his. "Shh. Calm down." He kissed my lips easily and then leaned down so we were eye to eye. "I won't work for my dad no matter what. But it doesn't matter, because we aren't going to be fired. Alexa won't say anything. You can talk to her tomorrow. Explain. She's supposed to be your friend. She'll understand."

I shook my head. "You heard her. She's angry. And she's been talking about getting an AM fired for weeks now."

He opened his mouth, and then his expression softened. "Then so be it."

My eyes snapped up. "What did you say?"

"You're more important to me than the job. If she tells the partners and they decide to act, then okay. I can deal with that. I can find another job." He leaned into me, his forehead pressed against mine. "I can't find another you."

"I hate when you say things like that."

He gently touched my lips with his. "You love it. I want to be with you, openly. If there are consequences, so be it."

A smile tugged at my lips. "Openly?"

Aidan walked over to the kitchen counter and pulled something out of the basket he kept there, then returned and held out his palm to reveal a silver key. "I've been thinking all weekend long, I barely slept, and it occurred to me that I'm doing the one thing I promised myself I would never do—I'm letting my father control me. In an indirect way, but I've been so afraid that I'd become him that I shut down things I want in my life to prevent it from happening. But I'm not afraid anymore. Of him or of losing my job. The only thing I'm afraid of losing…is you."

My smile widened, unable to be contained now. "And that's…?"

"A key to my apartment. Take it or don't, the choice is yours, but it's an open invitation. I'm serious about us and our future. I want you and only you, Cameron. Tell me you want this, too."

I crushed my lips to his in answer, relief pouring out of me. Maybe everything would be okay. Maybe Alexa wouldn't say anything, and Aidan could talk to the partners. Maybe they wouldn't care.

Pulling away, I kissed him softly once more, then asked, "You really don't think she'll say anything?"

He nuzzled his nose against my neck, breathing me in. "I promise you, there's nothing to worry about."

Chapter Twenty-Nine

There are moments in life that seem to play out in song. You can hear the drumbeats when something exciting is about to happen. The slow song when you finally make eye contact with the guy of your dreams. And the horror music when you're walking to your doom.

I should have called in sick. Should have claimed to have the flu or pneumonia or the freaking West Nile virus. Instead, I took Alexa's smiley face reply to my text as a sign that everything was fine. But no, the little yellow emoticon wasn't smiling at me—he was laughing the wicked laugh of the evil. Evil who went by the name Alexa.

The office was too quiet, every head down, every set of eyes on their work. I'd never heard the office so quiet in all the time I'd worked there. Then my gaze shifted to the front desk, curious if Alexa had the nerve to show her face, but her chair sat empty, her computer screen dark. My heart sped up as I took a few steps toward the main hall, and then my eyes locked on Aidan's office. The always-lit, always-open office. But now, the blinds were closed, the room dark. I stared at it, unable to believe this was happening, and then I heard my name called from my left, and I peered over to see Gayle watching me, her expression unreadable.

"Cameron, can I see you in my office, please?"

And there went my stomach. So this was what it felt like to be fired. Through all this, I knew the risk, but deep down I never thought anything would actually happen. I thought I was safe, that Aidan would somehow protect me, like he said. But how could he protect me when he was as much at risk, maybe even more?

I swallowed hard and said, "Of course," before following Gayle to her office. She closed the door behind me and went around to her desk, her eyes on anything but me. That fact alone said enough.

"I trust you know why I asked you here," she said, her focus now on me.

I knew exactly why I was there, but I wasn't stupid enough to hang myself. "I'm sorry, Gayle, I don't."

The clock on her desk seemed to tick louder with each passing second, wearing me down. I wondered if Aidan was in a similar meeting with the partners. If he were getting fired this second, or maybe they just planned to fire me, though surely that wasn't legal. I'd never sue, of course, but they didn't know that and—

"Cameron."

I glanced up, my hands shaking. What would my father say if he saw me now? Would he tell me to be honest? Would he tell me to be strong? "Yes?"

"Can you tell me what happened? Or rather, how it

happened?" When I didn't immediately respond, she added, "I know about you and Aidan. He's in with the partners now."

My heart dropped into my stomach. There it was. The elephant in the room. And while a huge part of me was afraid, another part was relieved. I'd been carrying this secret for months now, petrified someone would find out. Until that moment, I never realized how much it weighed me down.

I met her gaze. "It started the Saturday before my first day." And then I told her everything, leaving out the personal details that were no one's business, but recounting the slow build of our relationship. More than once I found myself fighting a smile despite the situation. Aidan was a part of me now, and nothing that happened here would change that fact. I didn't regret him. I didn't regret us.

Gayle waited until I finished, then leaned back in her chair, her fingers drumming against her desk. "So, what you're telling me is that this relationship has been mutual from the beginning? At no point did you feel pressured to enter into this arrangement? You never felt your job was in jeopardy?"

My eyes widened as I realized what she was suggesting. "No. Never. Aidan spent the holidays with me and my family. This isn't an office fling. It's…I…" I couldn't bring myself to tell her that I loved him. Not because the words weren't true, but because I wanted him to be the first one to hear them.

She sighed. "Oh, Cameron. I was hoping you would tell me it was just a fling. That would make our decision easier."

"Decision?" Fear crept up my back once again.

"Our informant—"

"Alexa."

Gayle hesitated, but eventually nodded. "Alexa. She's claiming that Aidan showed you preferential treatment because of your relationship. She's demanding your job."

"What? He would never, and you know how hard I worked on the Blast account. Aidan had nothing to do with my success here." Did he? I thought through my time with Sanderson-Lowe. Aidan and I worked as a team, sure, but he didn't give me handouts. He didn't help me with my work.

"I believe you. I do. But her story is convincing. If you agreed to stop seeing each other, I could have you transferred to a different division to avoid any further conflict, but I'm guessing that isn't an option?" When I didn't reply, she sighed heavily. "I'm not sure what the partners will decide, but I feel it's best for you to take the rest of the day off. I'll let you know as soon as I hear something."

Disbelief coursed through me, numbing my insides. This wasn't happening. I'd worked too hard to get this job to see it pulled out from under me so quickly. "So, that's it then? I'm...fired?" Tears brimmed in my eyes, and I blinked hard to push them away.

Gayle's face fell. "I'll do all I can."

• • •

Four hours passed with nothing—no calls from Gayle, no emails. No hints at what was happening. And no Aidan.

I had hoped he would send me something, anything, to tell me everything would be okay, but my phone sat silent on the end table of my apartment. My mind drifted back to my graduation day at NYU, how certain I was of my life.

But then I met Aidan, and began working, and somehow

my ideals shifted. I still longed for that rush of success, but that was no longer the only rush in my life. Aidan made me feel things I hadn't felt in a long time, maybe ever. And with that small crack in my structured thinking, I began to see other things differently, too. My mom loved me, Eric loved me, and my family, while a shade past crazy, absolutely loved me. And I loved them. I wasn't sure if I would ever move home, but I was proud of my upbringing. Without it, I wouldn't be the Cameron I was today.

Now I paced my apartment, and everything had somehow flipped. I still wanted to be successful, but I now understood that my career wouldn't be defined by my first job, but the experiences over the course of my lifetime. This moment did not make or break where I would be in thirty years. But there was only one Aidan Truitt, and I loved him. I couldn't imagine walking away from him. Not now.

I had just decided to send him a text, my nerves unable to wait another second, when a soft tap sounded from my door. Reaching the door in three long steps, I yanked it open, already knowing who I'd find on the other side.

Aidan stared at me without moving for several seconds, his face etched with exhaustion and worry. I wrapped my arms around him and closed my eyes, breathing him in.

"How bad is it?" I asked, unsure if I really wanted to know, but I was an adult now, and adults were forced to endure even when they wanted to hide.

He kissed my cheek and then pulled away from me. "Let's talk."

A chill moved through me as I searched his face for a deeper meaning. "Talk?"

Aidan opened his mouth, then closed it back and looked

away. "Yeah, we need to talk."

I stepped back so he could enter and followed him over to my couch, simultaneously wishing he'd spill whatever he needed to say and then wishing he'd keep it to himself. The tension was too much.

"Do you want something to drink?" I asked.

His hollow eyes penetrated through me. "No, I don't want a drink. I want you. I've thought about everything, my father, my job, and I want you. And I have to know, I need to know, how much you want me back. How much does this mean to you?"

Fear ripped through me as I thought of how hard I'd worked all these years, and now, less than a year into my career, everything was falling apart. I thought of my family, how much they liked Aidan, how in every text or call with Mom since Christmas she asked about him.

But at the end of the day, I wanted Aidan more. People didn't end their lives and look at their first job as a benchmark on their life's success. They looked at the people around them, and I wanted him to be my person. The one there until the end.

I leaned forward, unable to stay away with such a sad look on his face. "Enough that I told Gayle I wouldn't end this."

"Enough that you would stay, be mine, even if I weren't here? Even if weeks, months passed without seeing me?"

"What are you saying?"

Aidan raked a hand through his hair and stood up, pacing the floor as I'd done just moments before. "They're making me choose—either you're let go with a generous severance or you get to keep your job...but I have to take over in London."

"No. They can't do that. You can't leave. We're just getting started. This…we…I'll just quit. I can find another job."

"They're holding to the non-compete, Cameron. If you quit, you'll be lucky to find another agency to take you on. Same for me."

"But what if I let them fire me? Doesn't that clear the non-compete?"

"Yes, but everyone in advertising will know why you were fired. This will wreck your career, and the partners know it. They're using this to their advantage to force me to go to London."

I started to say something else when I noticed the expression on his face. How did I not see it before? "You've already decided, haven't you?"

"What choice did I have?"

Tears brimmed in my eyes, threatening to fall, everything crashing around me. Either I kept my career, but the man I loved would be an ocean away, or I gave up my dream and his so we could stay in the city, together. "This isn't right. I won't let you do it. You said it yourself, your life is here."

"I care about two things, Cameron—advertising and you. I know this business, and you're a natural. I can't let you ruin your career because of me. I won't. I'm not my father. Through you, I've realized that, and as much as it'll kill me to be away from you, I won't be selfish with this."

I took a step toward him, searching my mind and heart for some argument, some response that could convince him that he was wrong. But there were no other options for us—the non-compete had our hands tied. This wasn't a situation where we could quit and find another job tomorrow.

We were locked out of advertising for a year if we left Sanderson-Lowe.

"I'll use Dad's money to float me while I search for another job. Something outside advertising. He would want me to use it for something important. Well, *this* is important."

Aidan shook his head slowly. "I can't let you do that. You should use it to invest in something, something for your future."

"I would be—us." But I could see the pain on his face. Using Dad's money would only make him feel guilty for causing me to use it. "How long do we have?"

His eyes met mine. "I leave in a week."

"A week?" The words barely escaped before I broke into sobs. Aidan pulled me to him and stroked my hair as I cried into his chest. Everything came back to me at once. The first time we met. That first kiss in the bar. The first time we made love. Each memory like a sharp stab to the heart.

"But I just found you."

Aidan walked me back to the couch and cradled me in his lap. "You're not losing me. It's only time. We can see each other every few months." The word held between us, just how long "months" truly was. I thought of the agony when he was in London before, and a strangled cry broke from my lips as I cried even harder. Months.

I'd finally found my perfect person, my other half, and now he was leaving. How would we survive that kind of separation? And then even if we were to get married, I'd have to move there, away from my family. I loved Aidan, but maybe love wasn't enough.

Chapter Thirty

I didn't want to go to the airport. I didn't want to say that final good-bye, kiss his lips one final time. I wanted to wallow in my bed for three weeks until he returned to me, but relationships were not solo things. He needed me to be there, to see him walk away from me, and so we walked hand in hand into the airport, my heart breaking little by little with each step.

Aidan didn't say a word the entire ride over, like there were no words for this, no speech that could make it all right. It wasn't all right. He was leaving, and I was staying, and nothing could ever make it all right.

JFK was as crowded as ever, the intense winter air outside making the airport seem even more cramped and hot. I yanked off my scarf, frustrated that I'd put it on, then my coat, then started for my sweater when Aidan stopped me. "I'm sorry."

I looked up at him. We were just outside security, as far as I could walk with him. "It isn't your fault I put on seven layers of clothing," I said, attempting to smile, but my mouth wouldn't quite work right.

He ignored my attempt at humor, his gaze on me, refusing to let go. "I'm sorry I agreed to London. I'm sorry I didn't try harder. I'm sorry I haven't told you a thousand times how much you mean to me. Because you do. You mean everything to me. And if you tell me you don't want me to go, then I'll stay. For you, I'll stay."

My gaze dropped, my throat closing up. I told myself I wouldn't cry here. That I would say good-bye to him with a smile on my face, a positive attitude…and then I'd bury myself in my bed for the rest of the weekend. But as I took in his misery, I couldn't keep my feelings hidden any longer.

"I don't want you to go. But I don't want you to stay, either. I know what that will mean to your career, and I can't do that to you. You're a legend, Aidan Truitt." I blinked away tears and smiled up at him. "That legend isn't dying today."

He pulled me to him, kissing the top of my head, then cupping my face with his hands, he pressed his lips to mine. "Three weeks?"

"It's nothing." It was everything.

"And we'll talk every day."

"Numerous times a day." And it still wouldn't be enough.

He checked his watch, the time looming closer to his departure. "I have to go," he said.

"I know."

"I don't want to go."

"I know that, too."

My heart sank as I peered up at him, wishing I could erase the sadness on his face, the worry lines that were etched around his eyes, the deep frown on his perfect mouth. "I'll miss you," I said finally, rising up to kiss him again.

"Every day."

And then our time had expired, and he walked away, disappearing in the crowd.

Chapter Thirty-One

I lay on my bed, Grace on one side of me, Lauren the other, while Richard Gere told Julia Roberts in *Pretty Woman* that the apartment was the best he could offer, and though I knew it was just a movie and life was so much more complicated, I couldn't help comparing it to my life. Because it had been two weeks since Aidan left for London, me standing strong at the airport while his plane took off, carrying him away from me. I didn't cry until I was outside, and then it took me another week to finally stop.

"I've seen this movie a thousand times, and every time, I get sad when 'It Must Have Been Love' starts to play," Grace said. "God, what a sad song."

The song began to play as if on cue, and Lauren reached for my hand, somehow sensing this could be my undoing.

"When do you see him again?" Lauren asked. She didn't look at me when she asked the question. She knew me so well.

"One more week."

"That's not that long."

It was an eternity. Already, the two weeks apart had been hard. I missed talking to him about my day, discovering his thoughts on new campaigns, watching movies and sleeping cuddled close. It was weird how we settled into our routines, how we grew comfortable with the people in our lives. So when they left, they took a little piece of you with them and you never felt whole again until they returned.

And that's where I was—a half person. Realizing the people in our lives were what mattered, not our jobs, not our successes. The people.

My phone vibrated against my stomach, and I peered down to see a text from Aidan, asking if I was around to FaceTime. We'd gotten into the habit of FaceTiming daily, and it helped. But it also made it worse.

Grace and Lauren waved that they were going to leave my room. The movie was over anyway. Richard Gere came for Julia Roberts, and they kissed, and all was perfect in the world. If only life could be so simple…

I answered the FaceTime call on the first ring, and there he was, in his bed, his blond locks messy and wet, and my heart clenched even tighter, my eyes burning, but I never allowed myself to cry on these calls. I didn't want to ruin the few moments we had.

"How was work today?" he asked.

I shrugged. "Same. Gayle brought in some new furniture company. Everyone's excited. Alexa quit."

"Quit?"

"Yeah, apparently the guys in creative were being mean to her."

Aidan smiled and settled further in his bed. "They always liked you."

I laughed. "Oh, I think this has more to do with loyalty

to you. Your replacement starts tomorrow. Ellen Price. They say she's cutthroat."

The call grew silent for a moment, the sounds of New York calling from outside, reminding me that I loved this city. I loved the constant feel that I was never alone. It was never quiet. The city was awake no matter what. But the comfort I'd always felt here didn't warm me like it should, and it occurred to me that everyone who mattered to me, beyond Lauren and Grace, was a plane ride away. Miles and miles and miles away. All for what? A job? A title? Suddenly those things no longer seemed like enough. Like Julia Roberts in the movie, I wanted it all. I wanted the fairy tale.

It took me a moment to realize I'd zoned out, that Aidan was talking, then I heard him say Ellen's name and noticed his tone had changed. "Sorry, what did you say?"

"Let me know how things go tomorrow with Ellen. Let me know if you have any problems."

"Why would I have problems?"

"Just…let me know."

I nodded. Great. If Aidan was worried, she must know our story.

Sighing, I tucked myself into my covers and closed my eyes. "I miss you."

He cleared his throat, and I opened my eyes, curious what emotion I would find, some hint at what he was truly thinking, but he just looked…sad. "Every day," he said, repeating what he'd said at the airport. "Cameron, I…" My eyebrows lifted, my heart speeding up as I waited for him to finish the phrase I longed to hear. The words I longed to say. But then he released a breath and said, "Sleep well."

I bit down on my bottom lip to keep it steady. "You, too."

Chapter Thirty-Two

I hadn't even set my bag down at my desk before a voice from behind me said, "Cameron, right?"

I spun around to a sharply dressed woman just outside my cube, her red hair pulled back into a tight bun, her expression unreadable. "Yes. Cameron Lawson. I'm an account manager."

The woman studied me, as though she expected someone else. Was she a client? Was she lost? Then she held out her hand. "I'm Ellen Price. I would love to speak with you for a moment if your schedule is open."

I straightened, remembering Aidan's warning from the night before. Ellen Price might think she knew my story, but I earned my place here, and I was damn good at my job. My relationship with Aidan didn't change that fact.

She closed the door behind her and sat down at her desk. "Cameron, I wanted to speak to you about Aidan."

Before she could say another word, I started in, anger

building in my chest. "Ms. Price, I have no doubt that you have an opinion, and I understand your hesitation, but I assure you, I am a dedicated employee. I will work hard. My relationship with Aidan doesn't impact my job. It never has."

Ellen smiled. "I can see why he's attached to you."

I froze. "I'm sorry, what?"

She leaned forward, her hands threaded on the desk in front of her—Aidan's desk. The thought made my heart tighten. One more week, seven little days. I could do this. "Aidan and I went to Columbia together. He recommended me for this position. He and my husband are old friends. We're happy that he's found you."

"Oh." Wow. This was not at all the conversation I expected. "Um, thank you. I'm sorry."

Ellen laughed. "No, I appreciate your drive. Don't worry, your relationship doesn't impact your role here. It doesn't define you."

I smiled at her, relief pouring over me.

We left her office for the morning meeting, and I forced myself to keep my head high, my face indifferent as Ellen called Aidan into a conference call for the meeting. One of our new clients was a large international food chain, which would require a unified campaign.

"Good morning," he said, the sound of his voice causing goose bumps to spread over my skin, my heart to become heavy. Even now, after all these months together, I was still captivated by his control in a meeting. No one oozed confidence and control like Aidan. He launched into the London office's role in the campaign, and then the call was over as quickly as it had begun. I fought the urge to ask him to stay on the line, to talk to us just a little longer. The room felt so empty without him there.

"Okay," Ellen said once Aidan was off the line. "Cameron, you'll be assisting Gayle and me with this campaign."

"Absolutely," I said, hoping my voice sounded more even than I felt. The last major campaign I'd worked on had been with Aidan. My mind drifted back to those first few weeks. We did make a great team.

The meeting ended shortly after, and Ellen patted my back. "It gets easier."

I glanced up. "What does?"

"The distance. My husband's a marine, so I know first-hand how lonely it can get. Let me know if you need anything." And then she disappeared out of the conference room, back to her office.

My phone buzzed with a new text just as I returned to my desk.

Aidan: *This is killing me.*

I placed the phone against my chest, then texted back.

Me, too. Can you move your meeting up so you fly home sooner?

Aidan: *My schedule won't allow it. Can you fly in for a long weekend? Hell, I'd pay for a private plane at this point.*

I grinned. *I hate when you say things like that.*

Aidan: *You love it.*

Me: *It's just one more week, right?*

Aidan: *You're right…*

Me: *I hate being right.*

Another boyfriend might ask me to dip into my dad's money, might even make me feel guilty that I wouldn't. But Aidan understood me and my reasons, which made me love him all the more. My chest clenched at the memory of us at the airport, the words right there, begging to be said. It was the movie moment, that scene where the lovers proclaimed their true feelings, and suddenly music began to play, and they kissed, and you knew everything would be all right. But as I stared at Aidan that day, I knew that wasn't our story. I would say those words and it would change nothing. He would still board the plane, and I would still be in New York, because that was life, and I didn't want to tell him I loved him under such depressing circumstances. I wanted to say it when we were both at our best, when the moment was alive with excitement and hope and joy.

Aidan: *So one more week, then?*

Me: *One very long week. Call tonight?*

Aidan: *I'll be waiting by the phone.*

I turned my phone off and tucked it into my bag, knowing if I didn't I wouldn't get any work done at all.

· · ·

I waited until Ellen left for the day and then slipped out, desperate to be alone for a moment so I could think. The frigid night air cut through my coat, while tiny snowflakes danced all around me. Tilting my head back, I allowed them to drop onto my face, basking in the magic of the snow in the lights of the city. Back home, it rarely snowed, and if it did, only an inch at best. But here, snow would continue until everything looked as though it'd been covered in white icing, and for a day it would be the most beautiful thing in the world. But then the snow became dirty slush, and there were no snow days. No calling into work because you couldn't get down your driveway. Though I wished we did have snow days, if only so I could spend the night talking to Aidan as long as he could stay awake, and then let his voice carry me off to sweet dreams.

An overwhelming sadness hit me, and I stopped walking. This was my life now. There wasn't an expiration date to this situation. No counting down the days and then everything would be fine. After these three weeks, we would have another three weeks, or a month, or two months. And then what? Would two months become six? I started to grab a cab and decided instead to walk around, to allow the city to distract me. But as I walked, memories would hit, one after the other, each playing out until finally I couldn't take it anymore and a sob burst from my lips. I had no idea how long I'd been walking, but my fingers and toes were now numb, my face tingly from crying, and I just wanted to go home. But not just home. I wanted to go home to Aidan. I wanted him to wrap me in his arms and stroke my hair until everything felt perfect again. But that wasn't my life anymore.

This was my life.

And now that I'd allowed the tears to begin, they wouldn't stop. I pushed into my apartment building, glad to be out of the cold, and then took the elevator up to my floor. As soon as I unlocked my apartment and the door was safely shut behind me, I slumped to the floor, my head in my hands, as I cried tears for everything I wanted in my life, and everything I now knew I would never have.

"Cameron?" Lauren said. "Are you all right? Did something happen with Aidan? Is that why he called?"

My head snapped up. "Aidan called you?"

"Yeah. I had a missed call from him, but he didn't answer when I tried to call him back. Then I called you and it went straight to voicemail. I was freaking out that something had happened. I almost called your mom."

"You didn't."

"No, but I was worried. Have you talked to him lately?"

"Yeah, I talked to him—wait, what time did he call? I haven't talked to him since this morning."

"Around noon."

My heart began to pick up speed, worry zooming through me as I frantically searched my purse for my phone. Crap. I'd forgotten to turn it back on this morning. I held down the power button, my hands shaking so badly I nearly dropped my phone to the floor. The screen came up, an image of Aidan and me in the background—and a plethora of texts and calls, all from Aidan. Without looking at them, I hit his name and jumped to my feet.

Something happened. Something was wrong, I could feel it. He would never call me so many times unless something had happened. I waited for the call to connect, but instantly it went to voicemail. I called again, and again, praying for a different response, but each time hearing his deep voice as he said his name.

Panic worked its way up my spine, crawling to each of my muscles until my entire body shook.

"Cameron, sit down before you fall down." Lauren led me to the couch, and I sat down, my brain searching for possible explanations as to why he would call so many times and not be available now.

The texts.

I started through them, each more disjointed than the last.

I need to talk to you. It's important. Can you call?

Cameron, please?

Call me?

Are you okay? Why aren't you responding? I'm calling Lauren.

Lauren didn't answer. Fuck it, I'm calling the office.

The admin said you left early. Please tell me you're all right.

I'm really worried here.

Damn, new admin! She doesn't even know my name. How would she know if I left early? I hit his name again, pacing the room as I worked my bottom lip between my teeth. Voicemail. Dammit. Frustrated, I threw my phone to the floor, then quickly grabbed it, checking to make sure I hadn't broken it, my mind whirling.

"What do you think happened?" Lauren asked.

I shook my head, tears burning my eyes. "I don't know. He's never like this. Something had to have happened, and now I can't get him on the phone and— What if he's been hurt? What if he was at the hospital when he called? What if he's in surgery now, and I have no idea what's going on and—"

Lauren pulled me into a hug. "No, honey, I'm sure it's nothing big. He just probably needed to talk to you, and now he's in a meeting."

"It's eight thirty here, and he's five hours ahead. He should be calling me or asleep. This…I can't just sit here." I spun around and started for the door, reaching down to grab my purse, my phone still in my hand as Lauren chased after me.

"Cameron, stop. Stop. Where are you going?"

"The airport."

"What? You can't go to the airport. Who knows when the next flight is to London? You could be there all night. Just stay here. Just wait."

"I can't wait here. At least if I'm there, I'm doing something. I'll worry myself sick if I stay here." I started for the door just as my phone rang in my hand. Without thinking I accepted the call and pressed the phone to my ear. "Aidan?"

"It's me."

"Oh my God. I was so worried. I thought…I don't know what I thought. God, I—"

A soft knock interrupted my rambling and for a moment I wasn't sure if it had been at my door or coming from the phone. I waited, and then the knock sounded again, this time clearly from both my door and through the phone.

"Aidan?"

I ran for the door and threw it open to find him standing there, cell phone to his ear. He slowly lowered the phone.

"Are you crazy—what are you doing here?"

"I had something important to tell you."

"What?"

"I love you." He took a step toward me. "I couldn't wait another moment to tell you, but then you didn't answer my texts or calls, and I thought something happened. And before I could convince myself to be logical, I had a plane ticket and was headed to the airport." Another step. "And that's when I realized that I didn't want to be an ocean away from you if something happened. I want to be right here, protecting you—loving you. I am in love with you, Cameron Lawson. Every fiber in my body aches when I'm away from you, and these last few weeks have been the worst of my life. I don't want to spend a minute without you, forget a day or a week or a month. And I know this is a lot to take in, but I can't do this anymore. Forget the job, I need you."

Tears raced down my cheeks, and before he could say another word, I launched into his arms, my lips on his, every emotion pouring out of me. I couldn't wait another second, because he was right. These weeks brought on a pain I hadn't felt since my dad died. An emptiness that couldn't be filled.

I kissed him harder, desperate to taste and feel every bit of him, then I pulled away. "I love you, too. And I don't want to do this either. I'll quit. I'll email Gayle tonight. I'll—"

"I sent my resignation in to the partners this morning."

"You what? No, you can't."

He peered into my eyes as he tucked a loose strand of hair behind my ear. "No, what I can't do is spend another moment away from you."

I rose onto my toes and kissed him again. "So you're here? For good?"

Aidan pulled me into his arms. "As long as you're here, I'm here. I love you. You're my home now."

And he was mine.

Epilogue

Eighteen months later

The DJ switched from the classic wedding dance songs to Frank Sinatra's "The Way You Look Tonight." I smiled as Lauren and Patrick went to the center of the dance floor. I had never seen her more beautiful or more genuinely happy.

The summer heat had worried me when Lauren selected July for her wedding, but like always, she had been right. A soft breeze blew through the air during the outdoor service, and when day turned into night and the candles were lit for the reception, I found myself dreaming about my own wedding. Or the hope of a wedding someday. Lauren's happiness made me hopeful in a way I had scarcely allowed myself to hope before. But now, here, watching her and Patrick dance, knowing that I was with someone I loved made me giddy inside.

I glanced around for Aidan. Ever since he quit Sanderson-Lowe and opened his own agency, he had been working around the clock, making calls, setting up meetings, expanding his business. Once the non-compete time frame lapsed, many of his main clients with Sanderson-Lowe followed him to his agency. At first, he worked out of his apartment, but then he took out a lease for a small office and hired Dorothy, his assistant from Sanderson-Lowe. Before long, his office became fully functional, complete with an art department and an account manager—me. We were living our dreams, together.

I had just started for the dessert table when a strong arm wrapped around my waist, pulling me back, and a deep voice whispered, "Dance with me."

"I was looking for you," I said, spinning in Aidan's arms.

"I'm sorry. I'm waiting on a call from an investor."

"Oh! That's wonderful. Who is it?"

"I don't know, actually. Which has me skeptical. Dorothy said he would be calling me today to discuss the terms."

We danced until the song ended, and then Aidan flashed me a guilty look. "Is it okay if I step outside for a bit? The call should come in any second."

I nodded. "Of course."

I waited until Aidan was out of sight, then walked inside the banquet hall to the bride's quarters and pulled out my cell phone from my purse. The time rolled over to 8:00 p.m., and I scrolled through until I found Aidan's name, then clicked call. The phone rang once before he answered with an urgent, "Are you okay?"

"Mr. Truitt. My name is Cameron Lawson. I would like to discuss Truitt Advertising, and my interest in becoming a silent partner."

I continued through the banquet hall, where we'd

enjoyed most of the reception, and out onto the front porch, where Aidan stood, a look of shock on his face. "You're the investor?"

Ending the call, I started for him, a smile stretching across my face at his expression. "I've spent the last two years trying to think of something worthwhile to do with Dad's money, something that would make me happy, but make sense financially. This is that thing. The firm's growing faster than our space can hold, and we need to invest in marketing efforts to better get our name out there. Let me help. I want to be a silent partner."

"I can't take your money."

"You aren't. I'm investing in the business. If it continues at the pace it's at now, I'll be able to replace the funds in no time."

Aidan worked his lip between his teeth, his eyes on me. "You've thought through everything. You're serious? I thought the call was Eric."

"Eric? My Eric?"

Aidan nodded. "We had actually talked about it over Christmas, but at that point, the business was just an idea, nothing more. He liked my concepts, so when I made the leap, he called me. I wasn't sure at first, so I thought he called back to try to convince me."

"Wow."

"I know." He pulled me close. "We were actually talking about something else, too."

"Oh?"

He lowered his head to my ear. "I asked him for permission to marry you."

I jerked back, suddenly wide-awake.

"Before you freak out," Aidan said with a laugh, "not to-day. Or tomorrow. Or even next year. I will wait as long as it takes for us to be ready. But I love you, Cameron. I love the way you refuse to sleep with your hair down. I love how you drink tea at night and coffee first thing in the morning. I love the soft sounds you make when you're watching a movie you especially love. I love everything about you, and I want you to know that I'm here, yours, whenever you want me."

I closed the distance between our lips and tightened my arms around his neck. "I love you. And I would love to marry you someday. Please let me do this for you. For us."

He kissed me again. "Well, since you'd be a partner in the business, it only makes sense for you to spend more time at my place. You know, make sure I'm working around the clock to return those funds."

I grinned up at him. "Are you asking me to move in with you?"

"I'm asking you to spend every moment with me, but I will settle for sleeping hours. I want to come home to you every day for the rest of my life."

"I hate when you say things like that."

"You love it when I say things like that."

My smile spread across my face. "I do." And then I press-ed my lips to his once again.

For a bonus scene between Aidan and Cameron, please leave an honest review on Amazon or Barnes & Noble, then email me the link to the review at kissingisalwaysallowed@gmail.com, and I will send you a bonus scene!

Acknowledgments

Thank you God for guiding me day after day.

None of my books would be possible without the support of my amazing agent, Nicole Resciniti. Thank you for always being there and talking me off the crazy ledge.

There were lots of hands on this book, and each person offered wonderful insight. The most influential, who understood the characters and gave this book her all, was my fantastic editor Kate Brauning. Thank you for your enthusiasm and advice and continued love of this story. It would not be half the story it is without you! And thank you to Liz Pelletier, Stacy Abrams, and Alycia Tornetta for offering early edits on the story and forcing me to push myself to make it better. I owe each of you lots of chocolate.

Behind every one of my books is the love and support of my family. Thank you to my husband, Jason, and my two girls for forever believing in me and for eating lots of takeout so I can do what I love. Thank you to my extended family, my parents, and my loved ones for making me feel accomplished even on my worst days.

Thank you to early readers of the book Siobhan Clayton, Kayleigh Gore, Jessica Mangicaro, Staci Murden, and Jennifer Jabaley. Thank you to Teresa Mary Rose and Jennifer Marmo for offering insights into all things New York. And a million thanks to Rachel Harris and Cindi Madsen for reading the book, for telling me you loved it, and for being such wonderful friends. I adore you both so very much!

Lastly, thank you to the Book Boyfriend Anonymous Facebook group, the Mel's Madhouse Facebook group, and all of my amazing readers. You are the reason I write. Hugs always.

About the Author

Melissa West writes heartfelt Southern romance and teen sci-fi romance, all with lots of kissing. Because who doesn't like kissing? She lives outside Atlanta, Georgia, with her husband and two daughters, and spends most of her time writing, reading, or fueling her coffee addiction.

Connect with Melissa at www.melissawestauthor.com or on Twitter @MB_West

Also by Melissa West...

Made in the USA
Lexington, KY
09 March 2016